FEAST OF PONTIUS PILATE

BY

E. ANN MCINTYRE

Acknowledgements:

Special thanks to the Online Catholic Fiction Group for their talented assistance with this book. I am in your debt.

Thanks to beta readers:

Sheila Richfield, author of *Wild Irises*.

Don Mulcare

Susan Peek, author of *Animals of God*.

"The Lord inconveniences us to make history! Those chosen by God to make history must take the problem on their shoulders, without understanding."

Pope Francis Mar 19, 2016

"In harbor, Caesarea

Congratulate me, my friend [Seneca], for I have reached my
'province.' Wish me a peaceful and uneventful term, without
rebellion, droughts or tumults, so that I may earn promotion
and in some higher post than this help to make history."

Pontius Pilate, 26 A.D (From the Letters of Pontius Pilate)

Part One
In Their Own Words

In This Time and Place

The Roman Province of Judea

18th year of Tiberius Caesar, Emperor of Rome

6th calendis of April

4th year of the 202 Olympiad of the Greeks

7th year of Pontius Pilate, 5th Prefect of Judaea, Samaria, and Idumea

Yosef Caiaphas, High Priest, and President of the Jewish Court of the Sanhedrin, at the pleasure of the Prefect of Rome

1. Jerusalem

Thursday, solis occasus [sunset]

On the road to Jerusalem

I HELD THE POWER OF ROME IN MY HANDS, and I relished putting it on display. My entourage traveled behind the standards of the Emperor, Tiberius Caesar. The Jews crowded the road to Jerusalem as they streamed toward their Holy City. People on foot dawdled. Their carts, sheep, and mules slowed our progress. The dust from the many hoofs and feet filled my eyes and throat.

"Cornelius, clear the road ahead before we choke to death," I demanded.

The soldiers chased the people and animals from our path so we could pass unimpeded. The braver Jews hurled curses at us.

My wife, Claudia Procula, traveling in her carriage squealed, "They are going to kill us."

"Hardly, my love. We are surrounded by soldiers."

I had grown used to the Jews' vehemence against me. I was not concerned about an attack by zealots. My men apprehended their leader, the murderer Barabbas, some days ago. I had already decided his fate, death by crucifixion.

On this occasion, our son Pilo accompanied Claudia in the carriage. His sixth birthday was in a couple of days. I glanced in the carriage. Pilo slept with his head on Claudia's lap, oblivious to the protests of the Jews.

We approached the city as darkness fell, just as I had planned so that our entry through the gates of Jerusalem would draw as little attention as possible. I ordered the standards lowered and covered. I discovered, when I first came to this province, that the Jews were sensitive to the display of images of the emperor anywhere in Jerusalem. That is a story I'd rather not repeat.

I did not know all the laws of the Jewish religion. However, it was in my best interest to avoid antagonizing them. The leaders of the Sanhedrin were capable of reporting my transgressions against their religion to the emperor. I had a few unfavorable reports. Any further missteps on my part could lead to an unwelcome retirement from my post, or worse if the emperor received such a report while not in the best of moods.

The walls of the city loomed against the darkening sky. As we passed through the gates of Jerusalem, the soldiers who stood on the ramparts above us snapped to attention, arms across their chests. The torches on the walls lit their faces. They looked fearful of me. Such an attitude kept them obediently under my command. No soldier wanted to be flogged or lose his head. I would not tolerate a rebellion from the Jews or their keepers.

I hated Jerusalem. The only time I went there was for the Jewish feasts. The population grew to over a million during Passover. How does one control that many people? As in other years, I expected trouble; someone was bound to try to repeat the Exodus with us Romans being the ones making an exodus. I had to maintain the Pax Romana, [Roman Peace]. I called in troops from every corner of Judea, Samaria, and at Herod's pleasure, Galilee.

We pulled up to the side entrance of the Antonia Fortress, one of many palaces built by Herod the Great. I dismounted to attend to Claudia's exit from her carriage. Because of his malformed foot, Pilo needed to be carried everywhere. I lifted him out of the carriage. A couple of our servants relieved me of him and carried him inside.

Commander Marcus Rufus, my Tribune and Chief Military Officer, who I inherited from my predecessor, Valerius Gratus, greeted me. He handed me a list of the cases requiring my attention.

"Your docket is full. Any crucifixions must be over and done by sunset tomorrow, before the beginning of Passover."

"Yes... yes, of course. How many?"

"Three for now, although Caiaphas asked us to assist with the arrest of a man they consider a troublemaker. I am preparing to send some soldiers with the Temple guards to take him to the Sanhedrin within the hour. They expect to bring him to you following their interrogation.

"That's odd. What's he done that they can't handle?"

"He went on a rampage in the Temple a few weeks ago."

"What did he do?"

"He threw the merchants and money-changers out of the Temple, overturned their tables…caused quite a mess."

"Did he kill any of our soldiers?"

"No, sir."

"Mount any attacks on our authority?"

"No sir, but he has been at odds with the priests. I witnessed him raging at them last week."

"I've been at odds with the priests. What crime has he committed against Rome?"

"I'm not aware of any, sir. According to Caiaphas, he could be trouble during Passover."

"Does he carry weapons?"

"No. He did enter the city on a donkey a few days ago. I received reports of people proclaiming him their king."

"He was on a donkey?"

"That is what I was told, sir."

"Are you…are you sure they weren't mocking him?"

Unbelievable. The Sanhedrin report problematic men, they don't bring them to me. I only convict those who committed crimes against our laws or presented a grave threat to our security. I wonder what they wanted me to do with him?

"Listen, we are tired after the long journey, and we need to eat supper. I will discuss this with you in the morning. I certainly am not going to hold court proceedings tonight. I don't care what Caiaphas has planned."

Commander Rufus snapped his heels together, pulled his right arm across his chest, and bowed his head. "Yes, sir."

"Oh, sir, before I forget, you should know Herod is in the city. He came earlier today."

"Thank you, Commander. See to it we don't encounter each other."

"Yes, sir."

2. The Upper Room

Fourteenth day of the Month of Nissan

The fifth day of the week after sundown

The Upper Room, in the Zebedee House, Jerusalem

"The one who has dipped his hand into the bowl with me...."
Mt 26:23

MY MOTHER, HER SISTER SALOME, the widow of Zebedee, and Mariam of Magdala, had prepared the Passover table as I had asked them. Mother was somber. Her eyes downcast. She knew something wasn't right. I did not want her to come to Jerusalem for Passover; she insisted. *Mother will need her sister.*

"Please, son, why now? It is days early," Mother whispered to me.

"This is as it should be. All must be accomplished. Please go with Salome this night."

Mother's eyes searched mine for answers. She ran her fingers down my face. I smiled at her. She frowned. She didn't accept my attempt to lighten the mood. I kissed her face. Mother turned and went downstairs with Salome.

Mariam of Magdala hesitated at the top of the stairs and sat down.

"Please, Master, may I stay?" she said.

I nodded. Mariam had been with me since I drove out the evil ones who possessed her. She provided support for my mission. Her faith in me was stronger than that of the men, save John.

I led the celebration of the Passover feast with my friends, one last time. We danced as we sang the Song of Moses. With the scroll in hand, I proclaimed the story of the Exodus, recalling how God freed us from the bondage of slavery in Egypt. When I finished reading the Sacred Scripture, we sat at the table.

The Passover Seder was before us, the lamb was roasted to perfection, and the unleavened bread was still warm. The sweet and bitter spices were ready for dipping. A lamp burned in the center and at either end of the long low table. We sat on our cushions, as was our custom. I took my place between Simon Peter and John.

This Passover would be different from our previous celebrations of the feast. This was my Passover. My disciples murmured among themselves. They wanted to ask the obvious question but dared not, "*Why are we celebrating the Passover tonight, two days early?*" They would understand soon enough.

A large flask of wine was in front of me. I poured the first of the four ceremonial cups we would share. I leaned back against the wall.

"I have long wanted to share this Passover with you." All eyes were on me as I moved to the preparation area. I removed my outer robe, wrapped a towel around my waist, picked up the jug of water and the basin.

I turned to my chosen ones, my heart sank, the first was Judas Iscariot. I knew he schemed with the Temple authorities against me. Still, I loved Judas. I forgave him even before he carried out his treachery. I knelt before him and took his sandals off. Judas averted his gaze until the water splashed on his foot. His eyes briefly caught mine. The evil one had him. My loss. My soul ached for him.

I washed the feet of all my gather disciples, the last one was Simon Peter.

"Lord, are you going to wash my feet?

"You do not realize what I am doing, but later you will understand."

"No! You shall never wash my feet." He stood up and grabbed the water jug from me.

"Unless I wash you, you have no part with me," I warned him.

"Then Master wash me all over," he said as he handed me back the jug and sat down.

"That isn't necessary," I told him. I slipped his sandal off and patted his foot as I poured the water over it. Tears formed in his eyes.

I said to my friends. "What I have done, you too should minister to one another. This is an example for you to follow. Like me, you are not to be served but to serve."

I put my robe back on and continued with the Seder according to our tradition until I got to the final cup. I filled it with wine and set before me the unleavened bread. That night, I made a new covenant with my disciples.

I lifted my eyes to heaven and prayed, "I thank you, Father, for those you have given to me. I pray for them that they may hold fast in our love. Father, bless and make holy this bread and wine that shall become my covenant with them and all who believe in me through their words."

Tearing the bread in half, I gave a piece to Simon Peter on my right and John on my left. "Take and eat; this is my body. Do this in remembrance of me."

Wide-eyed, they passed the bread around, taking small bites each.

I took the cup of wine. "This cup is the new covenant in my blood, which is poured out for you."

Mouths opened. The room was silent. Their minds could not comprehend what happened. This was something that they could only know in their hearts. They passed the cup between them, each taking a hesitant sip of its contents.

I took a deep breath and fell hard against the wall. "My heart is breaking for one of you is about to betray me."

They all said at once, "Surely, you don't mean me, Lord?"

Simon Peter grasped my arm, looked me in the eye and declared, "Master, even if all these betray you, I will never betray you! I'll die for you."

"Die for me? Peter, I tell you before the rooster crows today, you will deny three times that you know me!" I squeezed his arm.

Simon Peter's face flushed. He shook his head, creased his brow, and moved away from me. John leaned against me and whispered, "Who Master? Who will betray you?

"It is the one who dips bread into the bowl with me."

I leaned forward, picked up a piece of bread, and dipped it in the sour sauce, as did Judas. John alone knew the answer to his own question. He glared at Judas.

"Go and do what you must," I told Judas. He squinted as he reached for his treasurer's money sack. He left his place and stepped into the shadows. I could no longer see him.

The door downstairs slammed.

3. Claudia

CLAUDIA, PILO, AND I SAT DOWN to a late dinner. I could see the weariness in Claudia's eyes. The crowded roads made the three-day journey from Caesarea to Jerusalem exhausting. We stopped at Lydia and Arimathea, which provided some respite.

We barely spoke during dinner. When Pilo's head drooped toward his plate. I lifted him off the lounge. He groaned and fell back to sleep. A male servant took him from me and put him in his room. Claudia went to attend to Pilo's nighttime preparations.

After Pilo was asleep, Claudia and I reclined on the lounge. The full moon occasionally peeked through the curtains as they waved in the gentle breeze. Claudia laid her head on my chest.

"Why do you have to crucify so many people?" she asked.

Now, I should tell you that Claudia has sensitivities with which some women are endowed. After we had married in Rome, I noticed that she had an eagerness for the Greek games rather than Roman games. She said that she preferred the Greek games because no one gets rewarded for killing another person.

We first saw each other at one of those games. I competed in an equestrian event. I, of course, triumphed and was awarded the prize by Claudia's uncle, a son of her grandfather Caesar Augustus. I told Claudia that I valued her most. It made her feel special.

"We crucify those who dare to challenge our authority in these lands, and those who commit murder, or steal from Rome. That's the way we deal justice, my dear."

"It seems so cruel. I see far too many crosses on the landscape. There can't be that many men who hate us."

"My dear, the Jews want us out of what they consider their land. They don't accept our rule. Some begrudgingly keep the peace, but there are those who never will, take the man Barabbas, he is dangerous."

"Still, I don't like it."

"Yes, dear, I know."

***

Claudia retired to the bedroom. A stillness settled over the palace, our servants had gone for the night. I feared our late arrival kept them here longer than they expected. I suspected they would probably demand more pay in the morning. Demand all they want; they would not get more money out of me.

I strolled into my office in the Praetorium just off our living quarters. My large desk had numerous scrolls stacked on it, no doubt grievances or issues of one sort or another such as property disputes, complaints of excessive tax, and unpaid taxes.

Passover was the favorite time of year for the zealots and insurrectionists to challenge the authority of Rome. Criminals such as thieves and murderers did their work among the population. Dealing with them would take up most of my time in Jerusalem. As the tax collector, mediator, and judge for the emperor, I did what I had to do to keep Judea peaceful.

I had command of about five thousand of soldiers throughout my territory, but it presented me with little opportunity to contribute to the history of the empire. According to my orders from Tiberius, I was to maintain a cordial relationship with the Jewish leadership and assist in the enforcement of their laws and Rome's at the same time. Together, not an enviable task for anyone and, at times, impossible.

I walked out onto the balcony just off the Praetorium; the full moon illuminated the courtyard below. The torches flickered in the breeze. I wrapped my arms in my cloak against the chill of the spring evening.

I had guests in my courtyard; some of the Jews thought of it as a safe place to spend the night. Visitors to the city during Passover pitched their tents and bedded down in just about any empty space they could find. I considered having the guards remove them, but that would have caused a noisy protest and woken Claudia.

To the left of the Praetorium was an open area known as the Pavement, so named because of the large stones that made up the floor. Beyond the Pavement stood the imposing temple. From my vantage point, I looked directly into the Court of the Gentiles, the largest open space in the Temple. I never set foot in it myself. Most probably, I would not have been welcomed to do so.

The Hall of the Sanhedrin, located at the far end of the court, was dark and quiet. Curious. Apparently, no arrest had yet been carried out.

I headed back into our residence. My thoughts turned to Claudia. Not many wives accompanied their husbands to such places. Tiberius had not intended for her to come with me, but Claudia remained determined to go where ever I went.

I admit I pursued her after my game-winning equestrian performance. Tiberius, who had authority over her, was not impressed with my determination to gain her affection. He knew what Claudia didn't know; I saw in her an opportunity to obtain a position of authority in the empire even though I am of the equestrian class. My game plan worked. She fell hopelessly in love with me. Fortunate for Tiberius that she did, otherwise, if the truth of her paternity were revealed, no man in his class would have her; Claudia is his daughter by a woman who was not his wife at the time. Claudia told me this secret. Publicly, Tiberius only claimed her as his niece.

One month after our wedding, the great Tiberius called me to his throne room. I anticipated a prestigious appointment. My friend, Praetorian Prefect Sejanus was a close advisor to the Emperor, promised to secure a governorship for me. I will never forget my inner rage when I opened the assignment scroll. I shook as I read the word *Iudea*. Tiberius ordered me to leave the next day sans wife. I knew at that moment exactly how Tiberius regarded me; not well.

Claudia would have none of it. She stormed over to the throne room and told Tiberius that she was going with me, and he wasn't to stop her. He didn't. After seven years together and a son born of her, I had a fondness for the emperor's niece, even with all her peculiarities.

A year or so after we arrived in Judea, Sejanus, who I considered my patron, was accused of plotting the overthrow of Tiberius. The emperor, who had been living on the island of Capri since I left Rome, had Sejanus and his associates executed. I thanked the gods I was in Judea. I am sure that is what saved me from the Emperor's wrath. Still, I dreaded each communication from Capri.

I built a small but elegant temple in Caesarea, which I dedicated to Tiberius Caesar. It was my hope that it will put me in good stead with the Emperor. The Jews met any attempt I made to honor Tiberius in Jerusalem, with unreasonable objections. I couldn't even hang banners with his name on them inside the palace. The sons of Herod, especially Herod Antipas, made sure of that. I had to take them down on orders from Tiberius himself. How did he find out about them before I advised him? I had my suspicions.

I needed to rise early in the morning to work through the trials and have the guilty men crucified and dead before sundown. Before I retired, I checked Pilo. I watched him as he slept. There were times when I felt sorry for him. He could not run, ride a steed, or play games with the other boys at school. I leaned down and stroked his hair. He didn't stir. I so wished that the physicians could find a way to straighten his turned foot.

***

As I slipped through the curtain to our bedroom to joined Claudia, I could hear her talking. She mumbled. I held my lamp over her. Her eyes were closed. She rolled her head from side to side. It was apparent that she was having one of her dreams that leaves her exhausted and upset in the morning.

She spoke, "No, no, not him."

I grabbed a pillow, threw it over my head, and tried to sleep. Sleep eluded me as I listened to Claudia weep.

Claudia's dream state got worse. She flailed her arms and hit me. *Time to wake her.*

"Claudia, dear, you're dreaming."

She woke, sat up, and stared at me wide-eyed. She pushed me off the bed and screamed.

"Get out of here, you monster!"

I ducked as she hurled her lamp at me.

She's still asleep. I attempted to crawl back into the bed.

"Claudia, please, wake up, you're talking in your sleep."

"No, I'm not. You killed him! He was a good man."

"Who? What are you talking about?"

"Get out!"

I grabbed a blanket and headed to the living area. Better the discomfort of the lounge, then bruised by my wife.

4. Let This Cup Pass

Gethsemane, Mount of Olives

Late evening

"Father, if it is possible, may this cup be taken from me…"
(Matt 26:39)

I PEERED OVER THREE SLEEPING BODIES on the ground. "Peter, James, and John, can you not stay awake with me?" John leaned up on an elbow and then fell back down, mouth open. *Too much wine.* I was alone. All of them were snoring.

I staggered to a nearby tree. My chest heaved. My heart pounded. The hour had come, the time of darkness. My soul torn because my work to bring my Father's love to everyone had barely begun. I loved my family and my friends. I loved life. I did not want to die.

Father, must it end this way? A Roman cross? Please no, it's too hard! Abba, Abba, let this cup pass from me.

Mad visions danced before my eyes. A sudden pain ripped across my back. My stomach churned. I clutched my aching hands. My head throbbed. The sweat poured from every part of my body. I reeled from it. I was freezing. My body shook. I wrapped my arms in my cloak. The darkness was closing in on me. I could hardly breathe.

"Run, you stupid fool. You don't have to die. Go to Bethany. Lazarus will save you. They won't find you there." The evil one urged me to abandon my mission. It was my decision, my life or death decision.

I turned to the only one I knew who could save me from death.

"Father, if possible, let this cup be taken from me. Yet not as I will, but your will," I pleaded. My Father does not wish this upon me. Death is not His doing. The officials around me were making their murderous choices. I could do nothing to stop them from carrying out their own wishes; they were free to do as they pleased with me.

"You can prevent this. Run to your friend Lazarus. You saved him."

"Remember three years ago when I offered you the whole world if only you would bow down and worship me? The offer still stands. I can get you out of this. I can strike down your enemies by making them kill each other."

More visions filled my mind. *There are hundreds, no thousands, no, no there are far more people than I could count reaching out to me. Their pleas fill my ears. They cannot reach me. I cannot give myself to them unless...I die.*

"I am the resurrection and the life." I told Martha. I must choose.

I closed my eyes. *Be still my soul*. Deprived of my Father's voice, I prayed.

I know you are there, Abba, even though I cannot hear you. I know you are not far from me. Abba, I trust you. I place my life in your hands. I breathed slowly but deeply. My body began to relax. With each breath, in the depths of my soul, I let go. I surrendered.

Your will be done.

The tears poured down my face. Exhausted, I leaned against a rock. Drained of my strength, I could barely focus my thoughts. I felt dizzy. The stars spun in the sky.

My Father sent spiritual comforters to me. They helped. My human comforters slept on the ground a stone's throw away. The time had come to wake them. I grabbed a tree limb to steady myself. My legs shook so much from weakness that I could hardly stand. Three of my disciples laid sprawled out on the grass nearby. I limped toward them.

"Peter! James! John! Can you not pray with me?" They barely stirred. *"Forgive them, Father."*

"See, even your friends don't care about you or what is about to happen. Want to wager they don't run for their lives? You'd lose."

"Deliver us from evil. Satan! Leave me!"

I could see the torches flickering through the trees. The cohort was coming for me with Judas in the lead. With my legs finally under me, I walked to meet them. I heard the scrambling of feet behind me. Judas stepped forward.

"Master." He kissed me on the cheek.

I held on to him. "You betray me with a kiss?" He pushed me away and stepped into the night. My heart sank.

"Judas," I called to him as I swallowed my loss.

I turned to the cohort of well-armed temple guards and soldiers.

"Who is it you want?"

"Yeshua of Nazareth."

"I am he."

Suddenly an unearthly scream came from behind me. Simon Peter had woken up. He lurched passed me brandishing a sword. He attacked one of the soldiers and cut off the man's ear.

"Enough! Put your sword away," I reached over to the injured soldier and healed his ear.

The cohort jumped back in a moment of hesitation, then they came after me. They bent my arms backward. It hurt. Some of the soldiers grabbed Simon Peter and John. James missed their grasp. He turned and ran. They seized Philip, but he ripped his clothes off to escape. The others followed him.

"It's me you came after. You've got me. Let the others go."

The Centurion nodded. In the dim light of the torches, we recognized each other. He was Gaius Marius, a childhood friend from Sepphoris. He creased his brow and shook his head at me. Not long ago, I healed his servant because he believed I could.

The soldiers released Peter and John. My other disciples disappeared into the darkness, some in the direction of Bethany. Lazarus, Martha, and Miriam had guests that night.

Centurion Marius got off his mount and took charge of me. "I'll take him."

He bound my hands in front of me. The bindings were so loose I could have lifted my hands out of them.

"Our orders are to take you to the house of the High Priest. What did you do?" he whispered.

I appreciated his protective stance with me. "Be careful. Do not put yourself in danger for my sake."

Gaius pulled me closer to him as we made our way down the narrow path from the Mount of Olives.

I felt my inner strength return. I would need every ounce. Yosef Caiaphas was waiting for me.

Abba, it begins.

5. I Am

The House of the High Priest

"THE HIGH PRIEST ASKED YOU A QUESTION. Answer him!" The Temple guard hurled his fist on my face. The force sent me to the floor.

Yosef of Arimathea, my friend, rushed to my aid and helped me up.

"You cannot treat him like this. Yeshua has done nothing wrong," he said to Caiaphas.

"Well, we will find out, won't we? Bring the witnesses," Caiaphas demanded.

The guards dragged in a man, I didn't recognize. Terrified, his face bruised and nose bloodied, he fidgeted. I felt sorry for him. Money buys lies.

"Tell us what this man said about the Temple."

The witness shifted from one foot to the other. He did not lift his eyes to the council.

"He said he was going to destroy the Temple and rebuild it in three days."

Laughter filled the room. "Rebuild the Temple in three days, it took forty-six years to build!" they scoffed.

"He must have meant something else," Nicodemus countered.

I was grateful for Yosef and Nicodemus, seekers of the truth, they gave me comfort.

The Hall of the Sanhedrin at the Temple was where trials were supposed to take place. The Law did not allow trials to take place after sundown. Caiaphas knew it. Moreover, not all of the seventy-two members of the Sanhedrin were summoned. I saw John bring Nicodemus and Yosef. Besides them, I was not among friends.

They paraded in more witnesses. I barely listened as they eschewed my words to suit their own murderous intentions. They rushed witnesses in and out. Caiaphas wanted a swift verdict.

Yosef Caiaphas sat in his President's chair; he must have had it brought over in advance. This trial was well planned. His fingers tapped the arms. He glared at me with his eyes narrowed and his mouth pursed. He was getting ready to ask the only question that mattered to him.

Caiaphas adorned in his finest gold and crimson High Priest robes, stood and held out his hands to silence the members.

"Yeshua of Nazareth, we have heard many testify against you. However, these words of others do not alone convict. Therefore, I will ask you a question. The one you have raised in our minds because of the things you have said and done."

He placed his hands at the top of his robe just under his chin.

"I charge you under oath by the living God: Tell us if you are the Messiah, the Son of God."

Eyes closed, I prayed, *Father, I must proclaim the truth for you, and I are one*.

I stood straight and met Caiaphas' gaze. "I am. And you will see the Son of Man sitting at the right hand of the Mighty One and coming on the clouds of heaven."

Gasps filled the room.

Caiaphas ripped his robe. "This is blasphemy! What need do we have of more witnesses? He has condemned himself by his own words. What verdict do you all have?"

Shouts for my death came from all sides.

"Guilty! He deserves to die."

"But, under the Roman rule, we do not have the authority to put a man to death," others declared.

"In the morning, he goes to Pilate," Caiaphas said as he slammed his gavel on the table beside him.

The Temple guards grabbed me and hit me wherever they could. I tumbled to the floor. The kicking began in earnest. The pain ripped through me as their beating rained down on me. Yosef and Nicodemus pushed their way through the guards and, once again, rescued me from my tormentors' hands.

Nicodemus helped me to my feet and held on until I could stand. Yosef was on my other side, he wiped the blood from my mouth. I spit out a tooth. He whispered to me, "There is nothing that Pilate can possibly condemn you for. We'll be there with you."

The guards dragged me outside. Simon Peter stood by the fire in the courtyard. He shouted at a woman, "I swear I don't even know this Yeshua of Nazareth, you speak of."

A cock crowed nearby. Peter's head snapped in my direction. We locked eyes. His mouth opened, and his eyes widened. His face coiled with denial. He turned away from me and ran from the courtyard.

They hauled me to the back of Caiaphas' house where there was a series of small cisterns, one had a lock and chain hanging on the door handle.

***

"Abba, it hurts to even breathe."

If I could just sit down. "Excuse me, rats, I need to rest." I felt the furry creatures at my feet. I reached for the wall, with my hands bound in front of me, I eased myself down. Another sharp pain shot from my ribs to my back. Tears formed in my eyes.

"Abba…," *breathe. Easy now, breathe. Never thought something so natural could hurt so much. It's dark, and it stinks in here.*

"Abba, why can't I hear you?" Silence. "Abba, please, I need you." Nothing, I heard nothing but the slow drip of the cistern water and the scurry of rat feet. "Abba, I can't feel your presence." He always speaks to my heart. How can this be? I have always felt my Father's presence. "Abba?"

The rats squealed at the sound of my plea.

"Ouch. Rats go away; I'm not for you to eat." I needed to sleep and forget my ribs.

"Master, are you in there?"

John's voice echoed through the window. I stood by sliding up the wall to the small slit. I could just reach the bottom sill.

"John, I'm here. Are you alone?"

"Yes. I slipped by the guards."

"Be careful, John."

"I have a blanket and some water. Your mother asked me to bring them. Can you reach the window?"

"I think so. My hands are bound, but I can move them. How is Mother?"

"Better than I am," John replied.

"I need you to be strong, my friend. Is anyone else at the house?"

"Peter, but he is inconsolable. He is up on the roof and won't come down. My mother and Mariam are there of course."

"Be kind to Peter and pray for him."

"Master, I put a cup of water on the ledge."

As I reached up, the pain from my ribs shot through me. I gripped the cup. My hands shook. I couldn't hold it. The cup fell to the floor.

"I lost it, John."

He let out a groan. "Here's the blanket."

I pulled it through the slit. It fell to the floor, but I manage to hang on to an edge.

"I have it, John. It will help keep the rats off my feet."

"Masters Yosef and Nicodemus told us that Caiaphas has nothing for which Pilate can convict you. They think Pilate will release you. I pray they are right."

"John, will you take care of the women? It would be best if you can keep them from coming to the trial tomorrow."

"Master, it will be difficult. I don't think I can keep them away. It was hard to convince your mother to stay at the house tonight. She wanted to come with me."

"I love you John, Shalom, try and get some rest."

"Shalom, Master. You try and rest too." John's voice cracked.

I swallowed hard. I worried about my friends.

"Father, I know you hear me. You have always heard me. I pray for those you have given me. Protect them from the evil one and keep them from harm."

I sat back down on the floor, this time with a blanket to cover my feet and legs. The constant pain in my chest gripped me. I rested my head against the wall. My eyes were swollen. I couldn't keep them open. My cheeks ached from the pounding. My tongue kept hitting a tooth that was only half attached to my jaw. I needed sleep. In the morning, I had an appointment with Pontius Pilate.

6. Questions

Antonia Palace, Jerusalem

Before Sunrise

I SLIPPED FROM THE LOUNGE. I didn't get much sleep in the night. Claudia probably didn't get much rest either. It was still early, so I helped myself to some leftovers on the table from last night's supper. Our servants would not be preparing breakfast for another couple of hours.

My manservant waited for me in the salon. Shaving was such a grueling process and, if you did not have a skilled servant, it could be dangerous. I've had my share of bloodletting close calls.

I laid face up on his table and extended my head to his left hand. He patted my face and neck with olive oil then steadied the razor in his right hand. My eyes closed, I could have gone back to sleep, but the scraping of the cold steel blade across my neck kept me alert. I managed to get through the morning's shave with barely a nick.

Next, I entered the gods' worship room. A flame flickered in the small caldron. I tossed some lotus flowers and incense on the fire. I made my homage to the gods as-brief-as-possible, just to keep in good standing; one never knows when one might need a favor. I put in a good word for the Emperor; I needed to stay on good terms with Tiberius – if that was even possible.

With my daily oblations completed, I headed to my office in the Praetorium. The light of the rising sun peeked through the curtains as I approached the doorway. I saw the silhouette of Commander Rufus standing in front of my desk; I wondered if he even went to bed.

"Good morning, sir. I trust you had a restful night."

"No, I didn't. I had a restless wife."

"I see sir," Rufus said as he cleared his throat.

"What do you have for me?"

"The Edict of Crucifixion scroll is ready for you to sign for Barabbas."

I unrolled the scroll and gave a brief read of its contents. "I'm delighted to sign this one. Leave it on the desk so I can gloat over it for a while."

"Here are the two for the other men. We caught the Syrian Jew Gestas, attempting to steal horses from the barracks. He stabbed and killed one of our soldiers. The other man, Dysmas, was watching out for him."

"I don't need to see these two. They are clearly guilty. They deserve to die. Next."

"That would be the group from the Sanhedrin, led by Caiaphas himself. They have one man to bring to your attention."

"Show them in."

"You have to go out to them." Rufus glanced over his shoulder at the group of priests huddled together outside in the Pavement area. He continued in a lower voice. "The Jews fear defilement if they enter a pagan court before their Passover, sir."

"Ah, yes, defilement. How does one work with such people?"

Commander Rufus and I proceeded to the Pavement area of the court. Yosef Caiaphas and the Sanhedrin priests, Pharisees, and Sadducees waited for me. Their faces stern, their eyes flickered nervously at the bound man, who stood next to the High Priest. The rising sun painted an orange glow on their faces, giving them a malicious appearance.

"Good morning, Yosef. You have someone you want me to see?'

"Yes, Prefect. This man, Yeshua of Nazareth, has been spreading false doctrine among the people and casting himself as the Messiah."

The man, Yeshua, appeared to have had a worse night than I did. His face was bruised and swollen. His eyes lids blinked slowly as though they were too heavy to keep open. He seemed strangely serene, for someone who might be facing death.

A young man stood behind the prisoner. Farther back, a few women and a couple of older Pharisees who I recognized as Yosef of Arimathea and Nicodemus from the Sanhedrin, stood in the portico at the entrance to the Pavement. They watched me, their faces were shrouded with anxiety. One of them, an older woman, wiped tears from her eyes, another woman clung to her,

"What has that got to do with Rome? I care nothing for your religious squabbles. Get out of here."

I turned to go back into the Praetorium when Caiaphas suddenly stepped in front of me. "You don't understand. He has been inciting the people. They have proclaimed him *King of the Jews*. Is this not a crime against the Emperor?"

"*King of the Jews*' you say. Hmm." I motioned to their prisoner to come with me to the Praetorium. Commander Rufus joined us, as did the young man. I sat on the edge of my desk.

"So, are you the *King of the Jews*, as Caiaphas has said?"

He did not speak. He looked me straight in the eyes. His penetrating stare unnerved me.

"Where do you come from?" I asked him.

Silence. His eyes remained fixed on me. I looked at Commander Rufus, then back at the prisoner. He was still staring at me. I felt a shiver go down my back. I shook my head.

"You don't look much like a king. How big of an army do you have?" I suppressed the urge to grin at him. *Some king.*

Again, he said nothing. Strange, he should have been pleading with me not to crucify him.

I proceeded to walk slowly around him. His eyes followed me. His filthy clothes reeked of rats. Moving closer to him, I spoke in his ear.

"Are you going to talk to me? Don't you know I have the power to put you to death or to set you free?"

Finally, he spoke, "You would have no authority over me if it had not been given to you from above."

"Yes, from the Emperor."

He shook his head.

"To whom do you refer?"

He gave me no reply.

This is pointless. I'll try something else.

"I heard that you caused a disturbance in the Temple. What was that about?"

He was back into his silent mode. He seemed somewhat odd, but hardly a threat to Rome. Usually, prisoners screamed their innocence at me. This man stood there like a dumb ox.

"What do you have to tell me about riding into the city on a donkey?"

Still, he said not a word.

"I prefer a good steed myself." That got a reaction. The corners of his mouth turned up slightly as he gave me a hesitant grin.

This isn't getting me anywhere. I can't figure out what he has done.

I walked back out to speak to Caiaphas, "Yosef, did you say he was from Nazareth in Galilee?"

"He is a Galilean."

"In that case, I will send him to Herod. Let him find a reason to condemn this man. Frankly, in my judgment, he has committed no offense against Rome."

"You must deal with him yourself, here and now!" Caiaphas demanded.

I waved off his banter and returned to the Praetorium. I wrote a note to Herod concerning the charges the Sanhedrin brought against this Yeshua of Nazareth and handed it to the centurion.

I was curious about the Sanhedrin's motives for seeking the death of one of their own. I motioned to Commander Rufus.

"I am sending this man to Herod. In the meantime, find out as much as possible about his activities. I don't want any surprises if Herod sends him back.

"Yes, sir. I will check with my sources in the Temple."

Rufus handed me a note.

"Sir, your wife gave me this to give to you."

I looked over my shoulder, Claudia stood in the doorway of our residence. She held her folded hands to her mouth. I read her message.

"My dear husband. I have been plagued all night with dreams about this man. I believe he is a good person, and you should have nothing to do with him.

Your dear wife, Claudia."

So, that's what was bothering her last night. I re-read Claudia's note. I was concerned. My wife was receptive to prophetic dreams and warnings from the gods. Such was her gift and my curse.

Claudia smiled, and her shoulders relaxed at the prisoner's exit from the Praetorium. I nodded to her. *I hope he won't be back. I was the monster in her dream last night.*

I finally sat down to the work at my desk. The Sanhedrin group milled around the Pavement. A few of them, including Caiaphas, went with the prisoner.

They all should leave, now.

7. Herod's Games

Herod's Palace

I GLANCED OVER MY SHOULDER AT PILATE AND HIS WIFE. He was fair with me, even though I wasn't exactly cooperative with him. I have seen his wife, with Joanna of Herod's court, at some of my gatherings. This is not going to be a good day for her. I prayed for both of them.

Abba, I know you are there even though you have shut the heavens to me. I pray for those who accuse me, and those who seek to set me free. Your will be done, Father, not my will or theirs.

Centurion Marius from Galilee led me by my right arm. John, my mother, Salome, and Mariam of Magdala walk on my left. Yosef and Nicodemus were behind them. The centurion moved me to the left side so Mother could touch me.

"My son, what have they done to you?"

"They were rough with me, Mother. I'm sore. Thank you for the water and blanket last night. Stay with John and please be careful."

"Why have they bound you? You have done nothing wrong."

"Do not grieve for me, Mother, but pray for those who have hardened their hearts to the Father."

"I will not leave you, my son," she said. Her eyes were swimming with tears.

"Yes, Mother. I fear your heart will be broken this day." She gripped my arm. If Yosef were here, he would protect her from what she would have to endure. It saddened me that I, her son, could not comfort her. At that moment, I missed both my Abbas.

It was a quick walk to Herod's Jerusalem residence. The man who killed my cousin, John the Baptizer, waited for me. *Will he want to serve my head up on a platter?*

Centurion Marius handed Herod the note from Pilate. Herod rubbed his eyes as though it was too early for him to be awake; he pondered what to do with me. "King of the Jews, are you? Hmm."

He looked me up and down, tilted his head side to side, and scrunched up his face.

"You don't seem like a king."

He called to one of his servants. "Bring a cloak fit for a king." He let go a hearty laugh as the servant threw a pure white cloak around me and stuck a reed in my hand in place of a scepter. Herod poked fun at me. I got dizzy from being spun around for all to see my "majestic countenance."

Father, I pray for Herod, too.

"Let me see a miracle or two. I've heard you can change water into wine. I could use some fine wine," he laughed and lifted his cup in my direction.

I refused to respond to his taunts. *No, Herod, I will not turn your water into wine.* He was already drunk.

Several members of the Sanhedrin had followed us. Caiaphas and the priests elbowed their way passed the people gathered around me. Mother squeezed my hand.

"This man claims to be our Messiah, calls himself a king. What is worse, he has declared himself the Son of God," Caiaphas told Herod. Herod was part Jewish but only when it benefitted him.

"Is that so?' Herod responded. "The only king in this room is me," he chuckled.

"Son of God? Don't make me laugh. Servant, another drink!"

Herod continued to taunt me. "Messiah!" he said as he feigned a bow.

His servant spun me around again, much to Herod's delight. He soon bored of playing with me and decided that since I was in Judea, whatever crimes I committed, I was under the jurisdiction of Pontius Pilate. So back to Pilate I was sent, majestic cloak and all.

8. What Has He Done?

The Praetorium

I FELT COMMANDER RUFUS HOVERING as I worked through the mounds of complaints, which had accumulated on my desk. "Yes, Marcus what can I do for you?"

I looked up to see that I had the prisoner back in my office. "Well, you're back. Herod didn't want to deal with you either, did he?"

Herod had his fun with the prisoner. "Nice cloak, tried to make a king out of you did he? Be grateful you still have your head."

The centurion handed me a note from Herod.

"I find that this man Yeshua of Nazareth has not committed any crimes in my jurisdiction that warrant the death penalty. Since his alleged crime is in Judea, he is yours to deal with. Thanks for your consideration of me judging this man from my territory. – Herod Antipas, Tetrarch of Galilee."

"Wonderful." I looked passed the prisoner at the growing crowd outside in the Praetorium. Crowds meant problems, and I didn't want any problems. It was time to have another chat with Caiaphas.

Back outside, I was face to face with a belligerent High Priest, who scuffed his feet against the stone pavement. His face set in what was becoming a permanent scowl.

"Yosef, neither Herod nor I find any guilt in this man. He has committed no crime against Rome worthy of death. Since his offense is against your religion, you deal with him yourself."

"Prefect, you know we have no authority to put a man to death. We consider this man dangerous and capable of starting a riot. We fear he will destabilize the whole region and riots will ensue."

"How is he going to do that? He has no armed men."

"Prefect, we know this man better than you do. I can tell you he is dangerous. He threatened to tear down the Temple and rebuild it in three days!"

"What? 'Rebuild it in three days'? Come on Yosef, he is humoring you!"

I could not help but laugh. Caiaphas hated the man. I was starting to find the whole thing amusing. I have to admit, I'd never seen Caiaphas so riled-up about someone, except me when I broke one of his invisible rules.

"What do you want me to do with him?"

"Crucify him," the gathered group of Sanhedrin members shouted.

"Why, I repeat, what has he done?"

"He breaks the Sabbath by healing people." Someone shouted from the group of priests.

"What's wrong with that?" I retorted.

"He heals by the devil."

"Look, even the gods of Rome give men healing power. It is not a crime. It is considered a good thing." Their accusations were getting desperate.

"Sir, if I may speak to you," Commander Rufus whispered in my ear.

"Yes, what is it?"

"Perhaps a little scourging would satisfy their thirst for this man's blood."

I hesitated. He did not deserve that either. Perhaps Rufus is right, so I relented and sent Yeshua to be scourged. I hoped that this punishment would end the madness. I have crucified more than a few men in my time, but they were, at least, guilty of some crime against Rome.

I sat back down at my desk and waited. The whack of the flogging startled me. The man's agonizing groans echoed through the Praetorium.

The young man, who accompanied the prisoner, stood against the wall, shaking and holding his hands to his ears. He slid down to a crouch position on the floor. Hands to his face, he sobbed with each of his friend's cry-outs.

This might be an opportunity for me to get some vital information about the prisoner.

"What's your name, young man?" He seemed more like a boy to me. He can't be twenty years yet.

"John bar Zebedee," he whispered.

"Tell me, John bar Zebedee, has your friend ever spoken against Rome?"

"No, sir."

Another groan echoed in the Praetorium. John buried his face in his arms.

"Has he ever counseled you or anybody not to pay their taxes?"

John didn't answer me immediately; he rubbed his face.

"No, sir. He said we should give to Caesar what is Caesar's and to God what is God's. We all pay our taxes."

"I see." *The prisoner tells people to pay their taxes. I'd be willing to bet the Jewish authorities aren't too impressed with that.*

"Sir, please don't kill him," John pleaded.

"That all depends on..."

"On what? He's done nothing against your laws!"

"Hmm, maybe or maybe not."

"Please, stop the flogging before they kill him!"

9. A Thousand Knives

I T WENT ON INTERMINABLY. *Father, please...*" The barbs on the whips dug into my flesh as they were dragged across my back. The pain seared through me.... My back arched, and my body swayed with each lash.

"*I can't stand.* My legs came out from under me. I dug my fingernails into the column where I was chained by my hands

They stopped. One of them checked to see if I was alive. Satisfied, he returned to his position behind me. I looked back at them as they readied themselves. I caught a glimpse of my mother. She leaned against her sister. Yosef of Arimathea held them both.

Father, please... don't let her see this...

"How many have we done? I've lost count." The soldier's voice interrupted my thoughts.

"I don't know...maybe twenty," the other soldier replied.

"Twenty more or so?"

"You start. We'll pick it up at twenty-one."

"..... *Father, how... much... more...*

The barbs struck me repeatedly as soldiers continued their rhythmic swings.

There can't be much... skin left on my back. I can see... can see pieces of me on the ground.

"Stop. I didn't tell you to kill him!" *Pilate's voice.*

I can't feel my legs. They cut me loose. I smashed to the ground. *Father, I feel nothing. I feel everything.* Yanked to a standing position, I staggered. Everything was spinning.

They were not finished with me. I saw a flash of purple. I was naked, except now I wore a purple cloak. Things twirled again, this time, I think they were turning me. I heard words like "majesty."

A thousand knives pierced my scalp.... The blood ran into my eyes. I couldn't see.

Bring him to me now!" *Pilate's voice again.*

They pushed me forward. Someone took hold of me. I heard a whispered voice. It was Gaius, the centurion, my friend. "Can you walk?'

"I can't see where I'm going. Will you wipe the blood from my eyes?"

He did. I could see.

One foot in front of the other. I couldn't feel the floor. *Stairs....*

"Can you help me get up these stairs? I think my knees are going to buckle."

Gaius put his hand under my arm and helped me up the stairs to a waiting Pontius Pilate.

10. Who are You?

"ECCE HOMO [Behold the Man]," I said, not in derision, but in awe. He looked majestic. He wore a crown of thorns, and was dressed in a purple riding cloth; that is not what I saw. I beheld a man whose entire countenance was regal.

There's something about him...

He had endured a severe beating. He could barely stand even with the centurion holding him. I had a knot in my stomach.

"I can't. I can't do this," I said aloud.

I went out to the Pavement to speak to Caiaphas. "I am going to free him. There is no guilt in him according to the law of Rome."

"You can't. This man has declared that he is the Son of our God! You cannot free him. He must be crucified!"

The son of their god?

Back inside, I put it to Yeshua, "Who are you? Are you the son of your God?" He gave me no answer. Although I barely gave worship to the gods, I did not want to burden myself with the thought of condemning a possible deity.

I slammed my hands on the desk.

"Answer me! Who are you? Are you indeed a king?"

"Do you say this from your own thoughts or is it because the priests have told you?"

"Am I a Jew? Look, your own people have turned you over to me. What have you done?"

"Mine is not a kingdom of this world. If it were my men would have prevented me from being taken. But my kingdom is not of this kind."

"Ah, so you are a king then?"

"Yes, I am a king. I came into this world to bear witness to the truth, and all who are on the side of the truth hear my voice."

"What is truth?" *Truth. I'm not in the mood for a philosophical discussion.*

I have an idea.

"Commander Rufus, isn't there a custom of releasing a condemned man to the people during this Passover feast of theirs?"

"Yes, sir, there is. What are you considering?"

"Let's make the people choose who should die this day, this man, their *King* or the dangerous felon, Barabbas."

"But, if I may say, sir, what if they choose Barabbas? What then?"

"How could they? He has murdered their friends and family, too."

I sent for Barabbas. Caiaphas waved to me, he wanted to know what I was doing. Commander Rufus went out to the Pavement to explain my decision to allow the people to choose a condemned prisoner to release for their Passover.

The High Priest flailed his arms at me. He was not pleased. Caiaphas gathered the Sanhedrin members around him.

He is up to something.

Commander Rufus brought Barabbas to my office. He shuffled in the leg chains. I had two prisoners stinking up my office.

All I had to do was to take both of them, Yeshua of Nazareth and Barabbas, out on the balcony and get the people to make the decision, which one of these two men do I crucify?

11. Pilo's Foot

PILATE HAD AN IDEA THAT HE THOUGHT WOULD CHANGE the outcome and free him from making the decision. *Father, I pray for those in whose judgment I stand. Do not hold the decisions they make this day against any of them.*

Pilate donned his formal judge attire. He looked official in his white toga rimmed in purple along with his chain of his office, a silver medallion of Caesar hung on it.

Barabbas stared at me for the longest time. He smirked. *Father, I pray for Barabbas that once freed, may he turn his heart and mind to you.*

Pilate led us out on the balcony to face the crowd. Not many people were in the courtyard. Most people were from outside of Jerusalem and were in the final stages of preparing for Passover. These early morning political theatrics were of little concern to the masses. My frightened friends were not there, save John and the women.

Mother, please don't stay. Take her home, John. I wished she could hear me.

"People of Jerusalem," Pilate addressed the people gathered below, "as it is the custom on the day before your Passover, I am offering to release one of these two condemned men. I am asking you to choose now, which one I should release to you. Should I release Yeshua of Nazareth, who you have called your King or this man Barabbas, a convicted murderer of your people."

Pilate did not notice the Temple operatives prompting and even threatening the people.

The shouts were isolated at first, "Barabbas." The number of individuals in the crowd who shouted his name increased. "Barabbas! Give us Barabbas!"

"What am I to do with your king, your Messiah?"

They shouted back even louder. "We have no king but Caesar! Crucify him! Crucify him!"

Pilate's eyes searched the crowd as if expecting a different response. He looked back at me and shook his head.

Pilate took us both inside. I prayed for him. He paced the floor. His plan backfired. Still, the final decision was his. Teeth clenched his jaw rippled. He briefly sat in his judgment chair. He got back up and continued to pace.

"I can't, I just can't."

"I'm releasing you," he said to me.

"The people demanded me; you must release me!" Barabbas screamed as Pilate headed outside to tell Caiaphas of his decision.

I glanced at John, who had dared to stay with me. He stood a few feet behind me; his face was tear stained. He trembled. My youngest apostle and friend was also the bravest of men.

I looked around the room. Pilate's wife Claudia stood in the doorway to their quarters. Her eyes were bloodshot; they beseeched me. She came to me and held a cold cloth to my swollen eyes and wiped the blood from my face. It felt good.

"Benigne facis! [Thank you]," I said.

Her eyes filled with tears as she motioned to a boy in the doorway behind her. A servant held him because of his malformed foot. I smiled and granted her son the freedom Pilate's physicians could not give him.

He ran to me and wrapped his arms around my legs. His father's blue eye stared up at me.

"Go inside with your mother," I told him.

"Thank you, thank you," Claudia said.

Caiaphas' words to Pilate echoed in the Praetorium, "If you let him go, you are not loyal to Caesar. I will tell him that you are, in fact, a traitor."

12. Politics

I WAS IN SHOCK. CAIAPHAS WOULD DO IT. All it would take was another letter to Tiberius to ensure I lose my head. I couldn't face Yeshua. I couldn't look at anyone. I leaned against my desk with my back to the prisoners. Two scrolls were in front of me, one writ certified the crimes and punishment of Barabbas, the other the crime and punishment of Yeshua of Nazareth. The choice was mine and mine alone. My head was pounding.

I had commanded troops in battle. This judgment was harder than sending troops to their death. That was war; this… madness.

My gut told me Yeshua was innocent of their claims against him. Barabbas, on the other hand, was guilty of multiple counts of murder.

It wouldn't take much for Tiberius to convict me of treason. It's this Yeshua or me.

"Commander Rufus, release… release, Barabbas. And then get me some water in a basin."

"But sir…"

"I said release Barabbas!"

Barabbas strolled out of the Praetorium to the Pavement and passed the priest and the women. He was gone.

We'll get him again, I swear. I slammed my hands on the desk.

Commander Rufus brought me the basin. I stepped out on the balcony and said in a loud voice. "I wash my hands of this man's blood; I find no guilt in him. Take him and deal with him yourselves."

Back inside, I sat down at the desk, and without looking up, put my signature to the scroll with Yeshua of Nazareth's name on it. Commander Rufus poured a portion of warm wax on the scroll. I pressed it with the seal of my ring. I could not look at the prisoner.

The door to our residence slammed. *I've lost Claudia. I am a monster.*

Yeshua's voice broke the awkward silence, "The one who brought me to you carries the most guilt."

I looked up at him. *Who is this man?* Our eyes met. I saw only compassion in his.

Coward. My inner voice condemned me.

I had one more official act; I needed to write the charge on a sign to be hung on the cross over the condemned man's head. Commander Rufus handed me the signboard. I pondered as to what to put. *He hasn't done anything.*

My eyes focused on the crown of thorns on his head, it finally came to me, I wrote in three languages, Latin, Hebrew and Greek, *Yeshua of Nazareth, King of the Jews.* That's treason against the Emperor. Explains my decision nicely. Not exactly the truth, but…it will do. I showed him. His face lightened. I admit he was getting to me. I liked this Jew. I don't like many of them, but I liked him.

Damn coward.

I handed the sign to the centurion; he frowned. He led Yeshua away. They stopped near Caiaphas. He called me.

What does he want now? I went outside to meet with the High Priest.

"You must change that sign. It must read, He *claimed* he was King of the Jews not he *is* King of the Jews."

"Yosef, the words I have written stay the way I have written them. Do I make myself clear?"

***

I watched from the balcony as the centurion loaded the crossbeam on Yeshua's shoulders.

His knees briefly buckled. The weight of it always surprises the condemned. Yeshua looked over his shoulder at me. I turned away.

"I came into the world to bear witness to the truth, and all who are on the side of the truth hear my voice." His words echoed in my head. Who is he? I wish I knew.

It was only the third hour, and I still had to face my wife. If she ever wrote to Tiberius about this, I'd be a dead man.

I hate Jerusalem

13. Crucify Him

The Crowded Streets of Jerusalem

"CRUCIFY HIM! CRUCIFY HIM!"

"He saved others, let him save himself."

Their words tortured my soul.

Unable to lift my head against the crossbeam, I could only see the worn bricks at my feet. I heard those who taunted me.

My flesh ripped and burned under the crossbeam. The splinters from the rough wood dug into my wounds. The beam pressed on the crown of thorns on the back of my head driving them deeper. The blood in my eyes obscured my vision. I couldn't see.

An outcrop of rocks caught my right foot. I stumbled and lost my balance; my knees smashed against the stones. I fell flat on my face. I heard a crack. My nose throbbed.

The ropes securing the crossbeam to my arms loosened. The beam bounced off my back and hit the ground. People scrambled to get out of the way.

Centurion Gaius reached down to me. "Can you get up?"

I nodded. "There's…there's blood in my eyes." I managed to get into a crawl position. Gaius helped me to my feet and wiped my eyes. He put his water flask to my lips. The cold liquid felt good.

"Thank you, Gaius."

"I wish I could stop this, Yeshua," he said as he wiped the sweat from his own face.

When I was in trouble, you gave me comfort. Thirsty, you gave me drink.

"Centurion, get that man moving!" Pilate's commander ordered from on top his horse.

Gaius went in search of the crossbeam, which had gone off to the side of the narrow street. He struggled to bring it to me.

I bent over. Every part of me hurt. I couldn't tell anymore what didn't hurt. Gaius laid the crossbeam back on my shoulders and secured it with the ropes. More splinters dug into my skin. I cringed.

I took a few deep breaths. *One foot in front of the other.* At least, I could see my feet and the ground.

Abba, the cross hurts. I am so weak. I don't know if I can make it. It's too...

My knees buckled. I was thrown on the ground again. The crossbeam landed in the middle of my back, pinning me. The crowd cheered. The *Hosannas* are long gone. Adoration has turned to loathing.

I could hardly breathe with the weight on my back.

"Get up!" The Commander's whip slapped my shoulder.

"I can't."

Gaius lifted the load off and, with a mighty pull, I was on my feet. "I'm getting someone to help him."

"I can do it." I leaned over ready to receive the load. It was on. I walked again. I managed to pick up some speed. I think the water helped. Gaius was in front of me now. I could see his feet so I followed him. As we made the turn out the city gates, my knees gave way. I hit the ground. The crossbeam came down hard on the back of my head and neck. My right arm was numb. I couldn't move it.

"That's it. You are not carrying that thing one more step. You'll never make it up Golgotha."

He was right. I needed help. *I must make it to Golgotha and right now, I can't move.*

Gaius hauled me to my feet; my right arm hung at my side. He leaned me up against a wall. He went to retrieve someone to help me carry the crossbeam. It gave me a chance to look around. Most of my disciples had vanished.

A few yards back, John, my mother, his mother, Mariam of Magdala, Yosef of Arimathea, and Nicodemus huddled together. Behind them was Miriam of Bethany. She cradled her alabaster jar. *Save it for my burial,* I had told her. Her face was gaunt.

It pained me to see them grieving so. Tears filled my eyes, not for me, but for them.

A group of six women, directly across from me, wept and reached for me. They were sheep without a shepherd to care for them.

"Women of Jerusalem do not grieve for me but weep for yourselves and your children."

A man with a scowl on his face came up behind me and picked up the crossbeam. I reached for part of it.

He shook his head. "I can carry it." His arm muscles flexed as he lifted the beam with ease onto his right shoulder. He was strong.

"Thank you, what is your name?'

"Simon of Cyrene."

"Bless you, Simon."

"I was ordered to…" Simon started to say. He took a long look at me. His angry face softened. He nodded. "You're welcome."

Free of the crossbeam, I was able to walk better. Gaius was beside me, holding me by my left arm as we ascended Golgotha. I finally got to the top where the uprights of the crosses awaited their victims. My stomach churned. I fell on my knees. I heaved until nothing came out.

Gaius helped me up. "Over here." I stumbled as he led me to the center upright.

Simon dropped the crossbeam on the ground. The two other condemned men tried to go back down the hill, but the soldiers dragged them to either side of me.

My body started to shake. *I don't want to die like this.* I held myself tight. *I don't want Mother to see me in this state. I don't want her to see any of this.*

"*Father, please, let me hear you. I need you.*" His voice was silent. "*Abba?*" I heard only the screaming words of condemnation from the crowd.

"Crucify him! Crucify him!"

"You saved others, now save yourself!"

"Get down and stretch out your arms," Gaius said.

I dropped to my knees. Gaius slipped my garment off, taking with it a good portion of skin. My whole body shuddered with pain. I am leaving this world the same way I came into it, with nothing on. I crawled to the center of the beam and rolled over on my back. I stretched my left arm out across the wood.

"I can't move my other arm," I told Gaius. He knelt beside me and placed my arm on the beam. The pain shot through me.

"It's not on your shoulder. This is going to hurt," he said as he pushed my arm into my shoulder.

"Ahh...Abba." I focused on my Abba.

"I can't do this," Gaius whispered. He had tears in his eyes. "One of the younger men will do it. Here, put this between your teeth. Not that it will help much."

I bit down on a cloth he put in my mouth and waited, eyes closed.

Abba, Abba, Ab...

Excruciating, bone crushing pain cascaded through my body. I shuddered as the iron bolts tore through both my wrist bones.

***

I opened my eyes, I was being hoisted onto the upright. The crossbeam slammed into the notch carved into the upright.

"Ahhh…" the jolt was violent.

Another sequence of bone crushing pain tore through my feet; more iron bolts. My body shuddered. My stomach heaved. I struggled to breathe.

Gaius was up on a ladder hanging the sign over my head.

"I thirst."

He put a sponge on his sword, dipped it in some wine, and put it to my mouth. I sucked on it. It was a mixture of sour vinegar, wine, and myrrh. Physicians used this combination to reduce pain. Gaius was trying to help me.

I love you, Gaius. My voice failed me. I hoped he knew. I turned down the gall.

Breathe. It was hard to breathe…hanging from my arms. I needed to push up with my feet. As I pushed, the nails rip further into my bones.

There is so much pain… I looked down.

Mother…I need to speak to her. I am all she has …older brother James is not her son. He's not obligated to care for her. John is here. It must be John.

I'll make it quick. Push up; breathe.

"Mother," her face filled with agony. I turned my gaze to John. "This is your son."

John's eyes were red. He understood what I was about to do. "Son, this is your mother." My mother is his mother. The quiet strength and gentle spirit she gave me will now be his, and be unto everyone who follows me. John pulled her closer to him.

My knees gave way. I lost my breath. I couldn't talk.

Abba! Abba, I need you. Why are you silent?

I gazed down at my friends gathered beneath me. I wanted to comfort each one of them.

The soldiers milled around as they tossed my undergarment between them. They gambled on it. Gaius grabbed it from them.

Push up, breathe. "Father, forgive them, they do not know what they are doing."

My legs gave out again. It got harder to breathe. I couldn't hold myself up. Short breaths, that's all I managed.

Abba, why have you abandoned me? I have done it all. Everything you have asked of me. Why do you leave me alone?

I pushed up and took a breath. "My God, My God, why have you forsaken me?"

It came out.

"If you are the Messiah, the anointed one, save yourself and us," the man on my left said in derision.

"Gestas, do you not know who this man is who is being crucified along with us?" The man on my right responded. "We deserve our punishment; this man does not. He is a good person."

"You're a dying fool, Dysmas," Gestas taunted.

I looked over at Dysmas. Our eyes met.

"Yeshua, remember me when you come into your kingdom."

With what little breath I had I said to him, "This very day, Dysmas, you will be with me in paradise."

The world started to spin. Darkness overtook the light. I couldn't see. I tried to breathe. No more pushing, I couldn't do it. I glanced at the sky. The sun was like blood. My chest was so tight, I couldn't…breathe. It felt as though it would split open. …my legs…my arms were ripping.

How much longer? …I can't breathe. Father…, please… take me.

I had to try….

Once more, push up, push up, breathe, "Abba, into your hands I give up my spirit… It… is… accomplished."

14. I am God of the Living

T HE SIGHT BENEATH ME WAS HEART
WRENCHING. I longed to wrap my arms
around my faithful ones who stood beneath my body. They
stayed when others ran. My mother had her head buried in
John's shoulder; Salome's arms were around both of them.
Mariam of Magdala was on her knees. She clung to the base
of my cross and wailed. Miriam of Bethany stood stone-
faced, staring up at my body. She quivered. Masters Yosef
and Nicodemus, the most learned teachers in all of Israel, did
their best to save me. Nicodemus covered his face with his
hands. Yosef stared up at me, his head shook from side to
side, his mouth trembled as the tears fell from his eyes.

The earth beneath them rattled. Frantic screams
emanated from the crowd.

The commander from Pilate's court sat on his nervous
mount as it bolted under him. He gave the sky an
apprehensive glance and reined his horse. He shouted orders
at the soldiers.

"The hour is late; they all must die immediately.
Break their legs, now!"

Two of the soldiers hammered the legs of Gestas and
Dysmas. Gaius stared up at my body. The commander yelled
at him.

"Well, Centurion Marius, he is your charge!"

"He's dead, sir."

"Prove it!"

My centurion hesitated. He looked back at my
mother. He motioned to John to block her view of my body.
John moved in front of her and pulled her face to his chest.
He reached for his own mother and put his arm around her so
she couldn't see what was about to happen. Yosef and
Nicodemus did the same for Mariam and Miriam. Mariam of
Magdala, however, struggled against Yosef.

"Spear," Gaius called to one of the other soldiers.

He glanced back at the women. He plunged the spear
into the left side of my body; it pierced my heart. Blood and
water flowed out. It was all I had left. John looked over his
shoulder and saw it. He closed his eyes. The tears poured
down his face. Mariam of Magdala collapsed in a heap on the
ground. Mother wrapped herself around John. Salome
grabbed her. The two sisters embraced. Their bodies
trembled.

My centurion friend, Gaius, stood behind my cross
near the edge of the hill. He threw the spear to the ground.
He lifted his head to the sky and said, "Surely, this man was
the Son of God." He fell to his knees. "What have I done?"

Greater faith in all of Israel, I have not seen.

At the bottom of the hill, Martha had arrived. She
struggled against the soldiers to get to me. Two other women
were with her, Joanna, a disciple from Herod's court and
Claudia, the wife of Pilate, she had her head well covered, so
as not to reveal that she was my disciple. Her husband did
not know.

Etched in my memory forever, the scene faded as I
slipped into eternity. Dysmas was with me. Gestas refused

my offer to join me. When the soldiers broke their legs, they couldn't breathe any longer. They both died shortly after me.

The horrific pain for Dysmas and me was over. The light; the glorious light of the Father enveloped us. My mission was completed, but my work of salvation for all was not yet over. I had to go to where the dead waited for me to free them and bring them home. Life everlasting was now open to everyone.

I am God of the living, not the dead.

15. Yosef of Arimathea

The Praetorium

DRAWN OUTSIDE BY A PECULIAR LOSS OF SUNLIGHT, I leaned against a column in the portico. It was mid-afternoon, the Ninth Hour, and it was dark as night. The eerie blood-colored sun cast a reddish glow on the empty courtyard. An earthquake shook the palace. I grabbed the pillar and held on in case the shaking got worse. It stopped. I felt an uneasiness in the pit of my stomach.

I was told later by Seers that these combined events were ominous warnings from the gods. They said the earth had shifted from day to night at that hour.

The residence door creaked behind me. Claudia peered out into the darkness that had descended upon Jerusalem. She covered her head and bolted from the Praetorium. I watched her run through the courtyard below. There was no doubt in my mind where she was going - Golgotha.

I ordered the guards to light the torches in the Praetorium and courtyard. The darkness lingered. My discomfort was growing.

From the portico, I noticed a single person crossing the courtyard in my direction. By his long black robe and white fringed attire, I could tell he was a Pharisee from the

Temple. Commander Rufus, on his horse, entered the courtyard behind him. He supervised the crucifixions.

I guess they are finished.

The shadowy figure of the Pharisee waited in the Pavement area at the entrance to the Praetorium; I assumed he wanted me to go and meet with him. I couldn't see him well, so I still didn't know who he was until he called to me.

"Prefect, I am Yosef of Arimathea, a member of the Sanhedrin."

I didn't know Yosef well, but I knew he was one of the oldest and most respected members of the Sanhedrin. He was not among those who were demanding Yeshua's death. He and another man, Nicodemus, stood with the women during the trial.

Interesting.

I made my way to the Pavement entrance. The Pharisee's face was glum. The amber light from the torches seemed to highlight the deep wrinkles in the old man's face.

"Yes, Yosef, what can I do for you?"

He barely lifted his eyes to mine.

"I have come to request custody of the body of Yeshua of Nazareth, so the family can bury him."

Commander Rufus stood to the left and slightly behind Yosef.

"Is he dead, Commander?"

"Yes, sir. The centurion ran a spear through to his heart. Blood and water came out, so he was dead before that. We broke the legs of the other men to hasten their deaths."

"Well then, Yosef, I will provide you with a note to give to the centurion." Back at my desk, and in the light of the torches, I wrote an order releasing the body of Yeshua of Nazareth to the custody of Yosef of Arimathea.

I handed Yosef the note. He turned to leave. "Yosef, if I may ask you a question."

He looked at me. I could see the sadness in his eyes.

"Do you believe that this Yeshua was your Messiah, the Christ?"

His shoulders sagged. He shook his head from side to side. "I had hoped. Unlike my colleagues in the Sanhedrin, I do not believe that the Messiah is to come as a political savior, but as one who conquers peoples' souls and turns their hearts back to God. Yeshua was just such a man. He did nothing to warrant this execution."

I shrugged.

"Then why? Why did you do as Caiaphas demanded?"

I was not willing to expose my inner conflict on this matter. "Caiaphas said that he was a threat to the peace and security of the region."

"A threat? A threat to whom, or what?" Yosef countered.

"To the Pax Romana, which I am sworn to uphold."

"Pax Romana? What on earth is that? Is the spilling of innocent blood the only way to keep this peace of yours?" Yosef pursed his lips. His white beard stood out against his flushed face, then he glanced at the steps leading to the Praetorium. Yeshua's dried bloody footprint covered the stone. Yosef's face softened. He looked me in the eyes.

"Before he died he forgave you and everyone who did this to him."

"He said as much before he left."

Yosef's eyes narrowed. I looked away from his penetrating stare.

"You are troubled by his death, aren't you?"

I gazed beyond the Pharisee at Commander Rufus. I chose my words carefully. "I did what I needed to do." I had another question to ask him, more out of curiosity than anything else. "Was he the son of your God?"

"He said *I am* to that question in front of the Sanhedrin during our so-called trial. That's why Caiaphas brought him to you. He used God's name for himself."

"What do you think?"

"I'm sorry Prefect, I have no answer for you." With that, Yosef of Arimathea turned and headed back to Golgotha.

Commander Rufus and I watched him go. "I'm glad this day is over. I have some making up to do with my wife if she is still speaking to me."

"Your wife, sir, is at Golgotha."

"I thought she might have gone there."

"She consoled the man's family."

"Oh."

"I have had reports that your wife was seen in Galilee attending one of the dead man's gatherings a few months ago."

I tried not to show my surprise.

"Why did you not tell me this before now, Commander?"

"I thought you knew, sir."

"She has not discussed the precise details of her visit to Galilee. I will attend to the matter."

"Yes, sir."

"Now, I must get some work done today." I turned back to my desk.

"Yes, sir. There is one more thing."

"Oh, Marcus, what is it?"

"Caiaphas has asked that we post a guard at the tomb of Yeshua of Nazareth."

"Why?"

"There are rumors that he told his disciples he would rise from the dead on the third day after his death."

"What superstitious nonsense. I thought Jews were abhorrent to such things."

"Wait, sir, there is more. Caiaphas is afraid that Yeshua's disciples will steal his body, move it somewhere else, and claim he has risen from the dead."

"I don't believe this. Is Caiaphas mad? The Nazarene's death is not enough for him. He has to chase him to the grave."

"Perhaps sir, but he is the High Priest and in Tiberius' good graces, and you, sir, dare I say, are not."

He does not need to remind me. Tiberius and his tolerance of the Jews will be the end of me yet.

"Oh, very well, proceed. Find a few guards with nothing else to do for the next few days and post them at the grave site, wherever it is."

"If I heard correctly, Yosef of Arimathea has offered his own grave to the family."

"Fine, dispatch the guards. Report any problems to me immediately."

"Yes, sir."

***

Back in my office, I stared at the closed door to the residence. Claudia hadn't yet returned.

If Commander Rufus was aware of my wife's attention to Yeshua of Nazareth, who else knows? This was a complication I didn't need. I could not allow my wife to be among the followers of a convicted criminal. She had not attended to her obligations in the worship room for quite some time. Was Claudia seeking after the Jewish God? I knew she had been with her Jewish friend Joanna a great deal. As a Roman, she must only worship our gods, not the Jewish God. Our law was clear in the matter; it only excluded Jews from having to worship the gods of Rome.

I'll have to confront her. The thought of putting my wife to death disturbed me.

I mindlessly shuffled the pile of complaints on my desk. I couldn't help but think of the earthquake and darkening of the sun. Were they just a coincidence? Or did they mark the time of Yeshua of Nazareth's death?

I'll have to make an additional offering to the gods tonight. Wiping my hands of that man's blood may not be so easy.

I heard a slight whisper of clothing; Claudia entered the Praetorium and, without looking at me, slipped into our residence.

This whole business is troublesome…

16. Alone

The Antonia Palace

I HOPE THE DOOR ISN'T LOCKED. I pushed. It opened. There was a pile of bedding on the floor in front of the lounge. The curtains of our bedroom were drawn and tied from the inside.

It's going to be another night on the backbreaking lounge.

The table had one empty plate on it, a half-eaten apple and a few grapes. Claudia and Pilo had finished supper. *I will dine alone this evening.* I reclined at the table and waited. I expected a servant would bring my supper forthwith. No servant came.

Surely, they don't expect me to get my own supper do they?

"Servant, where is my supper?" *Now, I am annoyed.*

"If my supper doesn't show up soon, I'm going to be angry, and no one wants to get me angry." There was no response from the kitchen. It's not that far. I knew they could hear me. Out of sheer frustration, I got up and went to the kitchen. No one was there. A plate of raw meat sat on the counter. The fire in the hearth was almost out.

I have to cook my own supper! This is unacceptable. Someone will account for this tomorrow.

I dumped the food on the plate into the over-sized pot hanging above the fire. I decided it needed more wood if I was ever going to eat. I stood arms folded looking around the kitchen, half hoping someone would show up, offer a huge apology, and cook my supper.

Wishful thinking.

The sizzle from the pot got my attention. The meat was burning on one side. *How do I stir it?* I cooked my own food on the battlefield; I searched frantically for utensils. There was no stir spoon. I took the pot off the hanger. The handle was so hot, I dropped it on the floor.

"Damn." I licked my roasted fingers. I grabbed a cloth from the counter and dumped the pot's contents back on the plate.

Someone is going to pay for this.

Back in the dining room, I ate a plate of half-burned meat. The pile of bedclothes on the floor by the lounge caught my eye. Claudia. Claudia has done this. She ordered the servants out. Now, what do I do? I can't punish the servants for following Claudia's orders. She, after all, is in charge of the kitchen staff.

The conversation I needed to have with my wife was not going to be an easy one. I suspected it was going to be a shouting match.

***

I threw the blankets on the lounge and attempted to get comfortable. I lowered the lamp's wick and closed my eyes.

The Nazarene's image appeared in a flash. I saw his bloodied beaten face and the crown of thorns on his head. My heart thumped in my chest. Sweat poured down my face. I bolted off the lounge and tried to calm my nerves. This never happened to me before. I never had a flashback to someone I had sentenced to death.

I paced the darkened room. I felt him. It was as though he was there. I turned the lamp up to dispel his ghost.

This is ridiculous.

I went to the Praetorium, I hoped the night air would calm my anxiety. The Writ of Crucifixion on my desk caught my eye. In the light of the torches, his name jumped out at me, *Yeshua of Nazareth.* He wasn't guilty of any crime against Rome, let alone treason. I studied it briefly. It troubled me. I did not need any more reminders of my botched judgment. I rolled it up. I had to send it to Emperor Tiberius. The three of writs would go with the next dispatch out of Caesarea, along with a full account of my judgment, carefully annotated of course. The Emperor demanded a full report on everything that happens in the provinces, and I mean everything. My reports were coming under rigorous scrutiny. The winds of political change were blowing in Rome and not for the better. I had to step carefully, so as not to further compromise my future.

I stared out at the now-empty Pavement area. The Nazarene's groans echoed in my head. *How could I let this happen? I am in charge, not Caiaphas. He had no business threatening me. That threat was all it took. I gave in, going against my own judgment.*

The bowl of water sat on the table in the portico where I disowned his blood.

"Dammit," I said as I smashed the bowl to the floor. The clatter echoed through the Praetorium.

A startled guard from below me shouted out, "Who's there?"

"Pilate," I responded as I leaned over the railing.

"Sir."

"Continue your watch, soldier."

"Yes, sir."

What is the truth? I asked him. He couldn't even give me a straight answer to that question.

"Anyone who hears my voice..."

I strolled back to the palace door, pausing to glance around at the Praetorium. Its emptiness and silence felt eerie. The light of the full moon illuminated the floor by my desk. Drops of blood and a bloody footprint caught my eye. Balancing the Sanhedrin's demands to uphold their religious laws versus the laws of Rome was not a task I'd wish on my worst enemy, or maybe, I would.

'King of the Jews,' – *may the gods save me from any more messiahs.*

I was tired. It had been an exhausting day. I dragged myself into the living area. The lounge actually appeared inviting. I flopped on it, hoping sleep would come. I rolled onto my side and demanded sleep from my body.

Sounds of sniffing interrupted a moment of slumber.

Is that Claudia? I listened. More sniffs. They were coming from Pilo's room. *What's he crying about? There are no servants here and waking Claudia might not be presently advisable. I better check, he might be sick.*

I rolled off the lounge, grabbed my lamp, and sauntered to Pilo's room. Curled up in a ball, he cried in his sleep. I pulled the covers up to his chin. Pilo's eyes opened.

"Go way... I don't like you!"

"Pilo, it's me Tata [Daddy]."

"Leave me alone. I don't like you!'

"Why?'

"Because...you...you killed Yeshua!"

"Pilo! I have a job to do. I must keep the peace in this land."

"You're an evil man! Go away."

I was shocked. What had Claudia done? I left Pilo's room and glared at Claudia's closed curtains. I had a mind to have it out with her right then and there but it was the middle of the night, and I needed to calm down.

Tomorrow is soon enough.

17. Did I Crucify a Deity?

Antonia Palace

Saturday Morning

MY BACK HURT. I got off the lounge and gradually straightened up. I needed to resolve the matter with Claudia as soon as possible.

Hand on my back, I limped into the kitchen hoping to find some leftovers. The meager supper the night before had my stomach growling. There was some meat stuck to the sides of the pot. I scraped it onto the plate I left on the counter. The meat was slightly burnt and crispy around the edges. It still smelled ok, so I figured it was edible.

Plate in hand, I wandered out to the living area and sat on the lounge. It was quiet, but I sensed I was being watched. Our bedroom curtains were closed. I looked in the direction of Pilo's room; he stood in the doorway.

My son is standing.

I glanced down at his feet. His left foot was straight. I quickly looked at his face, the tears poured down his cheeks.

"Pilo, your foot is normal." I rushed over and crouched in front of him.

"Yeshua fixed it," he said, as he wiped his face on his sleeve.

"What? How? When did he do that?"

"When he was all bloody and wearing the crown of thorns, and you were out talking to the priest. He just looked at me and smiled. My foot got straight. It didn't even hurt either," he said, as more tears cascaded down his cheeks.

"Oh my son, I didn't know...."

"Why did you kill him, Tata? He was a good man," Pilo said as he thumped his small fists against my chest.

Dumbstruck by the truth of my boy's words, I let my plate slip from my hand. It clattered to the floor.

He healed my son.

"I...I am so sorry Pilo, I really am," I told him. I ran my hand down his leg.

What have I done?

Pilo turned away from me, and ran back into his room; his curtain blew in my face. *My son runs. Pilo can run.* I felt my face burning.

I kicked the metal dish across the floor and went to the Praetorium. My stomach was churning. *He healed my son.*

Sunlight had begun to fill the sky. Splatters of dried blood on the floor caught my eye. I followed the gruesome trail out onto the balcony where bloody footprints marked the spot where I gambled the lives of two men.

'Shall I crucify your king?' I had to ask them, didn't I? Caiaphas and his gang of priests engineered the crowd's response. *'We have no king but Caesar. Crucify him!'*

What would have happened if I had let him go? Would Caiaphas have hunted him down? Well, he would have had someone else do the dirty work, but, yes, I think he would have killed Yeshua anyway he could. Mad men and their religions.

"Prefect –"

Startled by the commander's sudden intrusion into my silent ponderings, I turned quickly to face him.

"Good morning, Marcus. Glad somebody is still speaking to me."

"Not going well in the residence, sir?

"No." I decided to keep the details to myself.

"I have some items for your attention, sir."

I went to my desk and pushed the three Writs of Crucifixion aside.

Last night's cold supper was not sitting well in my stomach. "What have you got?"

"I have a list of people who have not paid their taxes."

"Is Yeshua of Nazareth on there?" I asked hoping that he did something illegal.

"Actually, his name is here with *paid in full* written beside it."

"Damn, worth a shot, though. How many are *not paid*?"

"There are fifty men and a couple of widows."

"I'll do up the warrants. Go after them starting tomorrow. Let them have their Passover."

"Yes, sir."

"Anything else?"

"No, that's it for now. By the way, you asked me to dig around and find out any information I could about Yeshua of Nazareth."

"What did you find?

"I heard something interesting. Last week he brought a dead man back to life."

"Oh, come on, Marcus, you don't believe that, do you?"

"Well, sir, Caiaphas himself was there. The man is Lazarus of Bethany, a priest, and a member of the Sanhedrin. He was apparently in the grave for four days. When Yeshua ordered them to roll the stone away, the air filled with the smell of decaying flesh."

"Isn't that the man we buy our wine from?'

"Yes."

"And he was dead and now he is alive because of that... Yeshua fellow?"

"Yes, sir."

Yeshua of Nazareth brought somebody back to life, did he? That is something only a god can do. Even I know that. No wonder Caiaphas was after him. Yeshua was one god too many for him.

"Thank you, Marcus, it certainly gives me something to think about."

"There's more, sir."

"Tell me."

"There was a blind beggar who used to sit at the entrance to the Temple."

"And?"

"He isn't blind anymore. Yeshua of Nazareth gave him his sight."

"And? Come on, Marcus, I know there's more."

"People knew that the man was born blind, but after the healing, he was dragged before Caiaphas and the Chief Priest who tried to discredit him… without success."

"So, this Yeshua did actually heal him."

"Yes, sir."

"The priests were outraged with Yeshua. They claimed that he did these things by the power of the devil."

"Aren't those good things? How can they claim he was bad?"

I felt as though every nerve in my body was shattered. Hands to my face, I leaned on my elbows. *I actually crucified a deity who also healed my son.* My stomach was in knots. *If he is anything like our gods, I could face serious repercussions. I had better go to the worship room tonight. I may need divine protection from the Jews' God. I have heard that he is revengeful.*

18. The Wrath of Claudia

Antonia Palace

Saturday, Early Evening

CLAUDIA STAYED OUT OF SIGHT MOST OF THE DAY; grieving or too angry to speak to me. It was supper time when she exited her room. Her eyes were red and puffy. She was furious.

"Yeshua healed our son if you care enough to notice!"

"Yes, yes I know. That's wonderful, but you cannot go around chasing after these messiah types. You are not a Jew. You must respect our laws!"

She spun around causing her long black hair to fly around her head and cascade down her face. *She's beautiful when she's angry.*

"I must respect the laws? What about you? How can you possibly claim what you did yesterday to be justice?"

Justice and truth are trumped by self-preservation. She should know that.

"Claudia, you of all people know that I cannot raise the suspicions of the Emperor, or he'd try me for treason. I had to crucify the Nazarene. Caiaphas demanded it."

There was a fire in her dark eyes. Her face flushed, Claudia pursed her mouth as she prepared to spew her words, as though she was a volcano spewing lava.

"I'm no fool. You took Yeshua's life to save your own. You are a coward. You can't even make a just decision when you should. You had the final say, not Caiaphas. Stop trying to shift the blame."

"Claudia, please listen to me. You are putting our family at risk by worshiping the Jews' God."

She paced around me like a cat encircling its prey.

"I'm putting us at risk? No, Pontius, you are! I'm leaving you. I have had enough of your brutal games. Yeshua is dead. You killed an innocent man. I leave tomorrow for Caesarea and from there we will go back to Rome. I'm certain Tiberius will have no problem granting me a divorce from you.

I'm taking Pilo with me, and you better not try to stop me," she said, as her right finger stabbed my chest.

She was determined. *How can I let her do this? How can I stop her? A man is a fool who lets his wife control his life, but...*

"I won't prevent you. But please let me ensure your safe travel by assigning some guards."

"Do what you must do to get our son and me out of this place safely."

Pilo will be six in two days, and I will miss his birthday. I will miss him. I execute one innocent Jew and lose my family. Damn it.

19. Heaven Is Open

In the Realm of the Dead

Since yesterday

"...in the spirit He went to preach to the spirits in prison."
(Peter 1:20)

I WENT TO THOSE WHO HAD GONE BEFORE ME to the netherworld to bring them my words of salvation.

"The way for you is open. Come, all you in the Valley of the Dead, come to me and through me to the one God and Father of the living. You are free.

"Adam and Eve, come, the key of my obedience has opened gates of paradise that were closed by your disobedience. To Abraham and Sarah, Moses and Miriam, and all the prophets, I say, come! Your salvation is at hand. You saw me before I was born. Now, come and receive that which has been prepared for you since the foundation of the world. Come!"

There was one person I sought, Yosef, my earthly father, a man full of faith and trust in God. He raised me as his own son. Formed me into the man I became. He taught me about the prophets and told me that when my Father called me, that I should face my future without fear.

He protected my mother and me from certain death. I will never forget the sacrifices he made. It was difficult for my parents living in Egypt away from their home. Yosef had to make a living in a land he did not know. In addition to worrying about me, he had left his motherless children with relatives in Nazareth, thinking he would be back from Bethlehem after the census. We spent nearly five years in exile.

Nazareth was a small town; the people knew before I did that Yosef wasn't my father. Yosef would have none of their wagging tongues about my mother, or the hurtful things others would say to me.

I remember the first time I attended the synagogue school; it was not long after we returned to Nazareth from Egypt. I was about six. The head rabbi ordered me out, called me a bad name, which the other boys repeated. I ran home in tears. I was devastated.

I didn't tell Mother because I knew it would upset her, so I went to Yosef's workshop, behind our home, and through my sobs, told him what happened. He threw his tools down and wrapped me in his big arms. "Don't tell your mother. I will take care of this."

I don't know what Yosef did, but the next day he escorted me to school. I stayed. Nothing was ever said again until I was much older and at the beginning of my ministry. That was when an angry crowd forced me to leave Nazareth for good. The people I had known all my life wanted to kill me. Yosef wasn't there to defend me. I lost him when I was thirteen.

He will always be my gentle giant, my foundation in manhood.

I greeted him, "Shalom, Yosef! Come home. The love and gratitude of my heavenly Father await you."

20. The First Day

The first day of the week

*"They will flee to caverns in the rocks and to the
overhanging crags from the fearful presence of the Lord, and
the splendor of his majesty when he rises to shake the earth."*

(Isaiah 2:21 JB Readers Edition)

A LL CREATION HAS LONGED FOR THIS
MOMENT. Since the beginning, when the first
stars shone and galaxies twirled, creation has waited. On this
the First Day, darkness becomes light. God's greatest
moment in time has come. Death is vanquished.

I am the First and the Last, the Alpha, and the Omega.

– Yeshua

Another earthquake rattled Jerusalem followed by
several aftershocks. Such was the power of my resurrection.
Transformed, my body slipped through the shroud and the
bindings.

I took a deep breath. *I am alive*! *Death is over, it no
longer holds me*.

The stone rolled away. My light dispelled the
darkness that held creation in its grip. I walked into my new
life.

A single soldier was flat on the ground. Gaius, the centurion, who believed, shielded his eyes from my light. His faith healed his servant. He walked with me to my death. He gave me a drink when I was thirsty. He witnessed my resurrection because he stayed; a courageous soldier.

"Such faith, I have not seen in all of Israel." I once said to him.

"Pax Vobiscum [Peace be with you], Gaius. Fear not, for I am the one who healed your servant. See and feel me. I am not a ghost, I am flesh and blood."

Gaius sat back on his knees as he reached out to touch me.

"My Lord, it is you!" Tears of joy streamed down his face. His pagan gods were dead because I am alive.

"Gaius, as you can see, I am dressed in the same manner I was on the cross. Would you have a robe I can put on?"

"Yes, absolutely, if you don't mind wearing something I've been using as a pillow." Gaius remained on his knees and crawled back to his crude bed. He held up a simple Roman tunic. I slipped it on.

"Thank you." I helped him to his feet.

He covered his face with his hands as he laughed from sheer joy. Gaius ran his hand down my arm. His fingers kneaded my flesh.

"You are really alive!"

"Go tell the authorities what you have seen, for you shall be my witness to them. In time, you will find John, the one who stood with me. Many will come to believe in me because of your faith."

Gaius headed toward Jerusalem, not wanting to take his eyes off me, he looked back over his shoulder.

The other soldiers were gone, but we were being watched. Commander Marcus Rufus from Pilate's court hid in the dark at the edge of the garden.

I must go. I have more people to see. The first is my mother.

21. All Things Are Made New

Antonia Palace

Before Sunrise

A N EARTHQUAKE SHOOK THE PALACE. I was almost thrown off the lounge. It was the second quake in three days. It felt stronger than the one on Friday afternoon. I heard loud crashes as things were thrown to the floor. My burning lamp fell off the table. I quickly smothered the small fire with my blanket. I tried to stand, but vibrations threw me back on the lounge. Finally, the shaking stopped. I sat and waited for a few moments. Out of the corner of my eye, I caught an odd white glow emanating from Claudia's bedroom. It did not look like fire. When I started to get up, the light disappeared. I shook my head. *I must be seeing things.*

"Claudia, are you alright?" She did not respond. I eased the curtain aside. It was dark, but I could see her shadowy figure sitting on the edge of the bed. She did not appear to be harmed, so I did not disturb her.

I turned to Pilo's room and pushed the curtain open. He was sleeping.

Concerned about possible damage to the palace, I hurried to the balcony to check the porticos. It was still dark, so it was hard to see beyond the light from the torches. The columns were all standing. Another smaller shake rattled the Praetorium. I sheltered against a wall.

I turned to go inside when I saw Claudia standing in the doorway. Her nightclothes blew in the light but cool breeze.

"My dear, it's too cold to be outside. Everything is fine. Why don't you go back inside?"

"Is he here?"

"Who my dear?"

"Yeshua."

"No. He's …" I didn't finish my words for fear if I reminded her that he was dead, it would unleash another round of angry words.

"He has made everything new again." She opened her arms wide as if to embrace the world. "All brokenness has been made whole."

"What dear?"

"A new day has come."

"Yes, dear Claudia. It is still very early. Why don't you go back to bed?" I suggested. I thought that perhaps she was sleepwalking in her dreams.

"I'll see you later," she said. Any hint of yesterday's anger at me was gone. I would know better in the light of day. She could be in a dream world.

I will await the dawn.

22. Mother

Jerusalem,

Zebedee House

The Upper Room

IT WAS STILL DARK; fortunately, the lamp in the corner of the room was burning. A full house of sleeping bodies occupied every available space on the floor. They all came back to where I celebrated the Passover with them. The air was stale from the windows being shuttered.

I stepped gingerly, taking care not to wake anyone. Simon Peter was in a corner propped up against the wall, mouth open and snoring. I remembered how that snore kept me awake some nights.

John slept curled up beside his wife, Mariam of Magdala. It was at their wedding in Cana that I changed the water into wine. Mother noticed that the wine was running low. She was worried that Mariam's family might suffer embarrassment if they ran out of wine. Mother expressed her concern to me, believing I would do something about the situation. I was reluctant. "My hour has not yet come," I told her.

I prayed to my Father for guidance. I received a 'yes'. I changed some jugs of water into wine. John and Mariam knew what I had done and believed in me.

Mariam stirred. I needed to find my mother. I thought that she must be downstairs with Salome.

Why do stairs only creak at night when everyone is sleeping and not during the day? I inched down the single flight of stairs.

Mother was awake. I knew she would be. Hands to her face, she rocked back and forth, as she prayed a mourning psalm.

I whispered, "Mother."

Her hands parted. In her silence, she opened her arms to me. I fell into them. We held each other in a moment of joy. She rubbed my face, patted my arms and kissed the wounds in my wrists.

"Yes, Mum, it's me. I am not a ghost. It doesn't hurt anymore."

She still had not said a word. Her face said it all. I don't think I've seen such a big smile on her face since before Yosef died. Her hands gripped my back. Mother buried her head in my shoulder. Her tears soaked my tunic.

"Stay with John. I will be returning to my Father."

She nodded and finally spoke in a whisper, "I love you, my son."

I wiped the tears from her cheeks and kissed her forehead.

The upstairs floor creaked. Mariam was awake and on the move.

I gave my mother another kiss. "I'll be back." I put my finger to her lips.

She nodded. She wouldn't tell, not yet. Her eyes glistened.

23. A Pleasant Breakfast

Antonia Palace

Sunday morning.

The 2nd hour

T HE SUN FINALLY DAWNED on the first day of the week. I had been up for hours. Claudia said yesterday that she would leave me today taking our son with her. After my encounter with her earlier in the morning, I was hopeful that she had changed her mind.

"Good morning, Pontius. Coming in for breakfast?" Claudia was up and still as cheerful as she was earlier.

"Good morning, dear. Yes, I would love to have breakfast with you."

Pilo was already at the table and happily eating his breakfast. Claudia and I joined him.

"I should tell you, Pontius that I'm not leaving you. I have decided to stay." Claudia's face was radiant. I wondered what transpired overnight that changed her attitude. Whatever happened, I am grateful to the gods.

"I am pleased to hear that, dear." I leaned over and kissed her cheek. Pilo laughed. I tousled his hair. He smiled and kicked both his feet on the floor. *Yeshua straightened his foot. Oh – there's that guilty feeling again. I have to stop thinking about him.*

"We can go back to Caesarea tomorrow. I expect to be finished my work by then."

"There's no hurry, dear," she replied. "Besides, tomorrow is Pilo's birthday, and we should celebrate here rather than be on the road."

Something was wrong. Yesterday, she was determined to get out of this place and away from me. Today, there is not a hint of her anger. Even Pilo grinned from ear to ear.

Pilo got up from the table and ran into his room. He came out peering from under a blanket he wore over his head. "I'm an angel, Tata!"

A child's pretend game. But where does he get the idea of an angel? Claudia must be feeding him Jewish talk.

Claudia put her hand to her mouth and laughed. I wasn't sure what to think. I shook my head and wondered if my family was crazy.

24. He Is Not Here

Just after sunrise

In the Burial Garden not far from Golgotha

MARIAM OF MAGDALA, MIRIAM OF BETHANY, carrying her alabaster jar of precious ointment, and Joanna approached my tomb. They came to anoint my body. They did not get a chance to do it before my burial, as Passover was fast approaching.

I waited and watched.

"How will we get the stone away from the entrance?" asked Joanna.

"I'm sure we can convince the soldiers to help. One of them believed in the Master," Mariam of Magdala replied.

The three women came to a halt when they saw my open tomb. Three figures in white appeared nearby. They were my messengers. Mariam of Magdala crept toward them. The other women followed her. Joanna had her hand to her mouth, as Miriam clutched the jar to her chest.

"Why do you seek the living among the dead? He is not here. He has risen." My messenger, Gabriel, told the women and then vanished. I smiled at the wide-eyed wonder on the women's faces.

Joanna and Miriam turned and ran back toward Jerusalem. Mariam of Magdala, however, stayed. She sat on the rock staring at the space where, just moments before, my messengers stood. Her eyes darted from side to side. Her chin trembled as tears poured down her face. She could not comprehend what had happened to my body. Mariam covered her face with her hands. Her shoulders shook. It was time for me to bring my friend from sadness to joy.

"Woman, why are you weeping?"

"I cannot find the body of my master. If you have taken him away and laid him elsewhere, please tell me," Mariam said, as she shielded her eyes from the rising sun. She didn't know me.

"Mariam. Mariam. Do not weep."

Her mouth opened. She lunged at me. "Master!"

I stepped back from her grasp.

"Do not hold on to me, Mariam, for I have yet to go to my Father," I said to her. "Go and tell my apostles that I have risen."

Mariam wiped the tears from her eyes, stepped back from me with her face beaming. She turned and ran toward Jerusalem; she looked back over her shoulder as she went. She will proclaim my resurrection to my apostles. They won't believe her without seeing for themselves. I'll just make them wait. Men don't acknowledge the testimony of women. Well, they should.

Mother will share Mariam's joy because she knows.

25. Kill the Rumors

The Antonia Palace

AFTER A STRANGE BUT PLEASANT BREAKFAST, I went to work. As usual, Commander Rufus was waiting for me in front of my desk. He looked a bit perturbed as he shuffled his feet. Head bowed, he nervously peered up at me.

"Good morning, Commander. What have you got for me today?"

"Not good news, sir." Rufus cleared his throat.

"What seems to be the problem?" *I've had enough mysteries for one day.*

"The body of Yeshua of Nazareth has been stolen, sir."

"What in the name of the gods happened? I had guards posted at his tomb." My face burned and my temples throbbed.

"Our guards at the site fell asleep. The man's followers seized the opportunity and removed his body to conceal it elsewhere," Rufus reported.

"What? They were asleep!" I slammed my fists on the desk. I couldn't believe it. "Does Caiaphas know yet?"

"He will know soon, sir. Rumors are starting to spread that Yeshua of Nazareth has risen from the dead."

Risen from the dead? I glanced back at the residence door.

"Kill the rumors whatever way you can*!" Caiaphas will rage against Rome's incompetence and demand my head.*

"Who was the soldier in charge at the tomb?"

"Centurion Gaius Marius from Sepphoris, sir."

"Has he gone back yet?"

"No, sir. I ordered him to clean up the crucifixion site."

"How many soldiers were at the tomb the last few days?"

"There were four of them, sir."

"Well then, those soldiers have a body to find, Commander. I suggest they get on with it."

"Yes, sir."

"And I want to see that centurion in my office before he goes back to Galilee. Such dereliction of duty under my command is unacceptable."

"Yes, sir."

I got up from my desk and headed for the portico. My headache was coming back. This was all I needed. I really wanted to leave Jerusalem before Caiaphas got wind of this. I leaned on the portico column, I heard Commander Rufus speak, "Sir." I saw a dark figure fast approaching from the Pavement. I turned around.

It was after Passover, so Caiaphas had no problem being in my office, and in my face.

"I hope you are satisfied with the work of your soldiers. Now the word is spreading that this Yeshua of Nazareth has come back to life. I swear Prefect; I will have your head for this." Caiaphas stormed out of my office. I didn't get a word out.

He will have my head. Of that, I have no doubt. Commander Rufus lifted his eyebrows as Caiaphas left the Praetorium. Then, he glanced back at me. I waved him out of the office. Rufus nodded at me in silence and left.

I heard the door to our residence close behind me. Claudia had been listening.

26. Bethany Friends

BETHANY, NESTLED IN THE EASTERN HILLS outside of Jerusalem, glimmered in the morning sun. Lazarus crouched in a small clearing at the top of the hill in the middle of his vineyard. He had been to the Valley of the Dead, now transformed into the Valley of the Living. He could hear the music and the angels singing. Lazarus didn't yet know why. Eyes closed, he listened to the chorus of Hallelujahs.

I knelt beside him. He was unaware of me. I whispered, "Lazarus." He didn't move.

"Shish…," he said. "I'm listening to beautiful music."

"Lazarus, it's me, open your eyes."

He did.

"Yeshua!" He opened his mouth, but nothing more came out. He wrapped his arms around me and wept hard. We had been friends since we were twelve years old. I had always been open with Lazarus about who I am. However, being the faithful priest that he was, he had never accepted it. Even after I returned him to life, he lived on the edge of doubt. Now I invited him to believe.

"Lazarus, do you now know who my Father is?"

He bent down and kissed my feet. Through his sobs, he spoke, "Adonai."

I was speechless. I waited so long for him. I lifted him to his feet. We turned to face Jerusalem and did what we had always done on this spot. We prayed the morning antiphons together.

We walked arm-in-arm down the path to the house, laughing at the strangeness of it all. We were both back to life with one exception; he would die again, I would not. I am the first to rise to the fullness of life. Someday, all will follow me.

"Martha! Lazarus!" Miriam's urgent call broke the morning stillness as she ran back from my tomb with her good news. Lazarus and I reached the bottom of the path just as Miriam flew through the courtyard gate. She saw me.

"Master, Master, it's true you are alive." She dropped her alabaster ointment jar, and she threw her arms around me. Lazarus caught the jar. Martha stepped out the door. Suddenly, I had two women hanging on to me. I stumbled to the ground. The women landed on top of me. Lazarus reached down, pulled his sisters off, and then hauled me to my feet.

We all laughed so hard we couldn't speak.

My friends were out of their darkness and into my light.

Martha was the first to recover her voice. "I'll get breakfast ready! Lord, you must be hungry after all you've been through."

"I can eat."

It was always pleasant having a meal with the Bethany siblings. Miriam grasped my left hand as the tears cascaded down her face. They were happy tears – I think.

Martha heaped the morning cakes in front of me. Then she laid out some fruit, and more fruit. Lazarus was missing a large bunch of grapes from his vineyard.

"Eat, Lord, eat," she said.

I couldn't help but smile at those two wonderful women.

Lazarus sat directly across from me. He was still shaking his head. His hand partially covered his face as he tried to hold back his tears. "How long has it taken me to believe you? You had to..." He buried his head in his hands. "Lord, I am so sorry..."

"Lazarus, you have been faithful to what you learned from your teachers. I have never asked you to be my disciple, only my friend."

"Can I be both now, Lord?" he asked.

"Lazarus, of course, you can. Indeed, you and your sisters will be great witnesses to me."

Lazarus, Martha, and Miriam had been my friends for many years. Lazarus and I first met when we were young boys and celebrated the Passover together with our families at the Zebedee house in Jerusalem. The Upper Room has hosted years of Passovers.

I had some unpleasant news to tell Lazarus and his sisters.

"My friends, I need to tell you something. It is necessary for you to leave Bethany; it is not safe for you here." My friends' happy faces suddenly became somber.

"Why Lord?" an astonished Martha asked.

"Those who sought my death also seek to end Lazarus' life. Your very existence, Lazarus, gives witness to me."

Lazarus stood up, rubbed his hands through his hair, and walked to the doorway. "Where shall we go, Lord? We only have this place and the vineyard." Lazarus lamented while he motioned to the vine-covered hillside.

I joined him at the door and put my arm around his shoulder.

"For now, you can hide at the Zebedee house. Caiaphas doesn't know we use it. It is best that all three of you go there. My disciples will make room for you. You are to remain there until I bid you go."

"When should we leave, Master?" Martha asked. Her face filled with anxiety.

"I suggest you wait until the cover of darkness before you go. Take only the minimal clothing and possessions. Turn your home and belongings over to your neighbor."

Miriam wept again. I pulled her head to my shoulder. Lazarus whispered, "I'm sorry."

"Lazarus, it's no one's fault, except perhaps those whose hearts are closed to the truth," I assured him.

This was difficult news; they had lived there all their lives. Martha has owned the house since their father's passing. Martha's take-charge personality emerged. She began to remove the breakfast dishes and give directions to her siblings.

"I can pack up our food. Lazarus and Miriam, you know what you need to take. This is difficult, Master, but we will do as you ask."

I hugged Martha. She will see her family through the difficulties that lie ahead of them.

I took one of Martha's cakes in hand, and I bid my friends farewell, for now.

27. Claudia and Joanna

Antonia Palace

Sunday afternoon

I T WAS MID-AFTERNOON when Joanna from Herod's court ran to the palace looking for my wife. She was excited and breathless.

"Prefect, may I visit with Claudia?"

"Yes, Joanna," I replied.

She rushed into our residence, leaving the door open. I leaned back in my chair to watch the two women. They were both excited. Claudia threw her arms around Joanna, and they sat on the lounge.

Curious, I thought, *Joanna was among those who followed Yeshua of Nazareth on Friday, at least from a distance. Why is she so happy?* I watched them for a while. Joanna seemed to be telling Claudia quite the story. I wished I could have heard what she was saying, but they were whispering, all I could hear were their giggles.

Claudia took Joanna to Pilo's room. Their laughter emanated from his bedroom.

Claudia was telling Joanna about Pilo's foot healing. Joanna had no doubt heard the rumors of the Nazarene's return to life.

Commander Rufus had not returned with any reports that the soldiers recovered the body of Yeshua of Nazareth. My discomfort was growing.

What would his followers have done with his body?

Is Caiaphas correct? Will they try to rouse the people to rebel against Rome? Perhaps they have another leader ready to take over the small group of the Nazarene's followers. They could grow in number if those people believe their crucified leader is alive.

I acknowledged Joanna as she left. "Joanna."

"Good afternoon, sir." She had a broad smile on her face.

"Give my regards to Herod."

"I will. Shalom."

"Isn't it a lovely day?" Claudia said as she stepped onto the balcony.

"Yes," I replied as I joined her and watched Joanna cross the courtyard. The sun was warm on my face, I squinted against its glare.

"What's going on? Is it still about the Nazarene?"

Claudia smiled at me and ran her finger across my brow. "Don't worry. You have nothing to fear from his followers or him."

"Claudia, surely you are not getting caught up in the nonsense fable about a resurrection? You were at Golgotha when he died. You know he is dead."

She pulled her shawl around her shoulders, looked at me but said nothing. She slipped back inside our residence.

The city was quiet, yet there was disquiet in my mind, uncertainty. I looked down at my feet. This was where he stood; an attempt to wash the blood from the stone floor failed. It almost looked fresh.

I hope those soldiers find his body soon.

28. The Pharisees

Somewhere in Jerusalem

NEXT, I VISITED THE TWO PHARISEES who stood with me during the Sanhedrin trial and took care of my body after my death. Nicodemus and Yosef of Arimathea were the only members of the Sanhedrin who did not want me to die.

I have known those two extraordinary men since I was a boy. They were Lazarus' teachers while he was preparing to become a temple priest. I met them during my first Passover in Jerusalem. They were such wonderful teachers that I stayed with them after Passover to hear more of their great stories. My family left that time without me. Easily distracted by all the things going on at the Temple during the Feast, I failed to notice that my parents had gone with the Zebedee family. They thought I was with all the other boys in the caravan. I wasn't. They had to go back to the Temple to find me.

Nicodemus was in his garden. I watched as he rocked back and forth chanting the psalms. I thought back to the evening he came to speak to me in secret. I told him that unless a man is born again, he could not enter the Kingdom of Heaven. Today, Nicodemus will be born again.

"Shalom, Nicodemus."

He stood, his face went white, fearful that I was a ghost.

"Fear not, it is I. See I am of flesh and blood as you are. I am not a spirit."

"Master," he said. He dropped to his knees.

I placed my hands on his head in blessing, then I crouched in front of him and held him.

Nicodemus embraced me and said, "My eyes see you, my hands touch you, yet how can this be so? We buried you."

"What does your heart tell you?" I asked him.

"Adonai, Adonai," he replied. He bowed low to the ground.

"Then believe that I have come from the Father and will return to the Father. All who believe in me will have life to the fullest."

"I believe, Lord. I believe," Nicodemus declared.

***

It was early evening when I went to the home of Yosef of Arimathea. He was in his study, poring over the ancient text of the prophet Isaiah. His reading eyesight was poor, so he leaned over the passages, nose to the script. He was unaware of my presence.

He prayed, *And yet ours were the sufferings he bore, ours the sorrows he carried, But we thought of him as someone punished, struck by God, brought low. Yet, he was pierced through for our faults, crushed for our sins. On him lies a punishment that brings us peace, and through his wounds, we are healed. (Is 53:4-5)*

Yosef wiped tears from his face. He held his head in his hands. It was time for him to know the prophecy was fulfilled.

"Shalom, Yosef. Fear not, it is I, Yeshua."

Like my friends before him, Yosef needed to touch me, hold me, and examine my wounds to ensure himself that I was alive in the flesh.

"How? How is it that you are alive? I…I…wrapped your body in the linen cloth and sealed the tomb. Master Yeshua … Adonai!"

He prostrated himself before me. I knelt with him and held his face in my hands.

"Whenever the story of my death and resurrection is told, Yosef, your kindness to me will not be forgotten."

I laid my hands on his eyes and gave him back the vision age had taken from him. He smiled, rubbed his eyes, and kissed my hands.

"Thank you, Lord," he said. "I so want to apologize for what happened to you at the hands of the Sanhedrin. They had no business…" I put my hand to his mouth.

"I have forgiven all of them who acted in such a way; the truth will prevail as it has prevailed in your heart, Yosef."

We sat together and shared our memories of our first encounter. He thought of me as precocious when I was twelve. He loved my questions. We laughed. It was his turn to ask questions.

"Master, are you now going to fulfill our hopes for the Messiah?"

"In God's time. For now, my words must go forth to the whole world, beginning in Jerusalem. I want you to take the Good News to all seekers of the truth."

Yosef will be one of those who I will send to the furthest parts of the Roman Empire. The old master is an excellent storyteller, a gift that will serve him well in his mission of spreading my word.

29. Shalom, My Friends

The Upper Room

BEHIND THE LOCKED DOORS and windows, they huddled together. Some waited expectantly, others were fearful. They had heard the stories. Mariam told them early this morning that I had risen, and she had seen me. As I expected, most of the men did not believe her. Then Lazarus, Martha, and Miriam came to the Upper Room and told everyone that they too had seen me. John knew it was true. He too waited. My mother sat quietly beside John, arm-in-arm with her sister Salome. Tears flowed down Salome's face. She didn't know what to believe.

Simon Peter sulked in the corner. He had heard the stories; even saw my empty tomb. His eyes drooped. He denied he even knew me. He was in darkness. He was in need of my light, my forgiveness.

There was a knock. Startled heads turned in the direction of the noise. Martha let out a squeal. Lazarus covered her mouth. James bar Zebedee held the 'shish' finger to his lips. They were fearful that it could be soldiers coming to arrest them. James inched to a crouch at the top of the stairs and listened.

"Shalom, it's Yosef and Nicodemus." A muffled voice echoed from the other side of the door. Relieved, James went downstairs and opened the door. The two Pharisees hurried up the stairs.

"He has risen! We have seen him," they breathlessly declared in unison.

Ten of those, I chose to be my apostles looked at each other. One priest and two Pharisees could not be making this up. The women hugged each other. My friends were now certain something had happened. Thomas was not there. I grieved the loss of Judas, if only he had waited.

"Why has he not appeared to us?' Philip asked the one question they all had in their hearts.

"He has abandoned us," Simon the Zealot said.

"Can you blame him? After all, we abandoned him. Just John, Yosef, Nicodemus, and the women stayed with him," James said.

"And you, Peter, there are tales that you denied you even knew him. That you denied him three times, just as he predicted you would," Nathaniel chimed in.

It was time to stop the blame game these men were so good at bantering about. It was time for me to visit my friends so that they might all believe.

"Shalom, my friends."

I stood in their midst. Mouths fell open. Those who had already seen me had broad smiles on their faces. James was the nearest one to me. He reached out. I extended my hand to his. We touched. Tears rolled down the face of the Galilean fisherman. He knew I was alive. He was on his knees as was everyone else in the room.

I lifted James to his feet. "Be not afraid, for I am with you." I moved around the room, greeting each person with the kiss of peace.

Simon Peter was still in the corner. He could not move forward and greet me. He was locked in his fear and shame. He had his arms wrapped tightly around himself. He barely looked up. I would have to make the first move.

"Shalom, Peter." I used the name I gave him because there will come a day when he will be a solid rock of faith. *Upon this rock, I will build my church.* This evening, however, he could barely lift his eyes to meet mine. I didn't push him. He will come around. We will meet again in Galilee. Until then I moved on and greeted the others who have been waiting.

On the far side of the room were my mother, my aunt Salome, and John. I had not spoken to John since I hung on the cross above him. He waited as I made my way toward them. John folded and unfolded his arms trying to contain his excitement. As I approached, he politely stepped back so I could greet my mother and his mother. Both women hugged me and then they moved aside.

"Master." John wrapped his strong fisherman arms around me. I held on to him, my faithful friend. Even at great risk to himself, he stayed with me. John's grip tightened. I felt him shaking. He was sobbing. It had been hard for him, I knew, but at that moment, his tightening embrace was hard on me. I had to tell him.

"John, I need to breathe."

Everyone in the room laughed. It was good to hear. It broke the tension.

"Have you got anything to eat?" I asked them. I can always eat.

Salome laughed through her tears and said they had some bread and fish. Yes, the Zebedee household always had fish. Too bad the late Zebedee himself was not there to experience that night. When I called his sons and their fishing partners Simon and Andrew to follow me, Zebedee suggested, firmly, that I should get my own sons.

I sat down to the meal the women quickly put together. I celebrated both my first and last Passover in Jerusalem in that room. The first Passover I had there was when James and I were twelve. I became friends with Lazarus that year. The three of us go back a long way. John wasn't born yet. He arrived three years later.

The room felt like home. It was right that my friends were there with me. I was touched by the love of all those gathered. I regretted having to leave them. However, I must. I had thirty-nine more days to prepare them for their mission on my behalf.

After the meal, Miriam of Bethany approached me carrying a bowl of warm oil. "Master, I didn't get a chance to anoint your body, so I was wondering if you would like a backrub."

"Yes, Miriam, that would be wonderful."

I stretched out on a bed my mother had prepared for me. Miriam took one look at my back, which still bore the wounds from the scourging and hesitated.

"Master, it looks so sore, I don't want to inflict more pain on you."

"It's all right Miriam. My wounds no longer hurt so your rub will be of comfort to me."

My skin melted under Miriam's healing touch. She gently ran her warm hands over my back, neck, and shoulders. Miriam rubbed my scalp. It felt good as her fingers massaged my head. The pain from the crown of thorns was now just a memory. With the warm oil, she gently pulled the knots of dried blood out of my hair. She hummed a sweet tune as she did so. Her long hair tickled my back. I remembered, how, in Bethany, at the dinner to which she was not invited, she rushed in and pour the expensive oil on my feet and wiped them with her hair. Miriam's kindness to me drew shock and anger from Simon, the dinner host, and his guests.

She moved her hands down my neck and shoulders. She carefully removed the embedded splinters with her fingers.

"Master, they must hurt."

"Not now."

Miriam worked the warm and fragrant oil on my back with her fingers and the palms of her hands, giving me a deep massage. Once the crossbeam burdened them, now, she made my shoulders feel light. My arms were next as she rubbed them with her palms. Her slender fingers interlaced with mine as she massaged my left hand and then my right hand between both her hands. She lifted a blanket over me. She was finished.

Out of the corner of my eye, I saw Miriam biting her lower lip as she sat back on her heels. There was a glint in her eye. She still had her cute girlish grin with dimples on either side of her mouth. The first time I saw those dimples I was twelve, she was nine, and Lazarus was a tease. Poor girl, she still blushes. Her dark hair framed her innocent face that belies the strength of her spirit. She believed in me before anyone else in her family.

When I forgave her sins, Lazarus, had a problem with it, as did others. Whenever her story is told, all will know that she has loved much. Miriam has chosen the better way, and it shall not be taken from her.

I drifted off to sleep.

30. Pilo and Mariam of Nazareth

The Antonia Palace,

Monday Morning

"*Come and see the empty tomb where I was laid after my death," says the Nazarene. I leave my room as though I am floating. It feels strange. He moves effortlessly ahead of me. Yeshua of Nazareth seems so alive.*

We stand at the entrance to the tomb. He invites me to look inside. I do. There is no body, only some blood soaked linen cloths.

"*See, I have risen."*

"*How can I be sure of this? The empty shroud means nothing. The soldiers claim your body has been stolen by your followers."*

"*You will know the truth soon."*

***

I SQUINTED MY EYES against the morning sun. I'd overslept. I had the oddest dream. Everything about Yeshua of Nazareth was odd. As I sat on the edge of the bed, I discovered that my back was no longer hurting. Claudia had finally forgiven me. I slept in the bed last night. I had my first good night's sleep in four days.

I could smell a breakfast of eggs and freshly baked bread. I was hungry. I heard Claudia humming. She was happy. *Happy wife, happy life. Was that Plato or my father who said that? ...cannot remember.* I peeked out the door; Claudia was putting my breakfast on a plate.

"Are you awake in there? Your breakfast is ready."

"Coming dear," I responded. *I wonder how long this good mood is going to last before it dawns on her that Yeshua really is dead. I had better eat fast, just in case her memory comes back.*

It was Pilo's birthday and Claudia planned a celebration at supper. Later in the morning, I arranged to surprise him with a ride in Jerusalem on my steed. I would go easy, of course, and hold on to him. He had never sat on a horse with a leg on either side so it would be a new experience for him.

***

Down at the stables, the centurion from Galilee attended to my steed. I wanted to ask him why he wasn't out looking for the missing body, but he was so helpful securing Pilo to the horse's back that I decided against upbraiding him then and there.

I'll deal with him later.

"I will come to your office this afternoon, sir. I have something to tell you."

"I just bet you do," I said to him, as I urged the horse forward.

"Happy Birthday, Pilo. Enjoy the ride with your father," the centurion said.

Cornelius and two other soldiers accompanied us for security. I did not tour Jerusalem without protection, especially with my son. We rode through the crowded marketplace. People jostled each other as they attempted to get out of our way. Some men lifted their fist to me, saying words I hoped my son didn't understand.

I didn't venture out of our palace very often in Jerusalem, but now and then it was good to see what my Jews were up to. They were shopping, cooking...smelled good whatever they were cooking, a few stalls away.

The market featured all kinds of interesting items. There was local pottery, potions promising eternal youth and both local and exotic clothing. Pilo was wide-eyed.

"Tata, can I have that?" he said pointing with glee at a plain white robe.

"It's nice, Pilo, but that robe is intended for a Jewish man," I told him. "We'll look for a small toga for you. I doubt that they'd have one here, but I will check."

"I want to give it to Yeshua."

What has he been hearing? Those women have my son confused.

"Well, son, I'm sure he would like it but..." I couldn't say it. I couldn't tell my son the truth. He would hate me, and I didn't want him to hate me on his birthday.

"Please, Tata, please. He will so like it. Besides, you got his other one all bloody."

I took a deep breath.

I'll just buy the damn robe and make my son happy.
Perhaps one of my Jewish servants will take it instead of pay.

With the robe secured on the back of the horse, we headed down a long quiet street that passed close to the Temple. As much as I would like to take Pilo in to see the Temple, I doubted that Caiaphas would have appreciated my presence in their sacred place.

"Tata, please stop," Pilo said.

"What is it, son?"

"That house."

The house Pilo pointed to appeared locked and shuttered.

"I don't think anyone is there, Pilo. They may have been there for Passover, but they have all gone home now."

Pilo continued to stare at the non-descript house. I urged the horse onward.

"No, Tata, please, he is there, I know he is. Please knock on the door and ask."

"Who is in there, Pilo?"

Pilo cocked his head around at me and said, "Yeshua!"

"Son, I really don't think so." I was not about to explain to him why not. I urged the horse forward.

"Tata, stop! Please!"

"Pilo. There is no one in there. They have all gone home." Pilo started to get off the horse. Fearing he was about to take a tumble, I grabbed him. "Pilo, stop it right now!"

Pilo looked back at me. Tears were pouring down his face. "Please, Tata"

Anything for one's son, right? "Alright son, I'll ask."

If people are in there, they won't open the door to Pontius Pilate, even if I am on a social visit.

I dismounted. Cornelius told me that he would make the inquiry. I said, "No, I will do it to satisfy my son."

"Who shall I ask for?" I pondered aloud.

"Yeshua, Tata," Pilo said from his perch on the steed.

I cleared my throat and knocked on the door.

"This is Pontius Pilate. I have my son Pilo with me, and he would like to see Yeshua," I said in my best Hebrew, trying hard not to laugh.

I waited. No response, just as I expected. I turned to leave when the door creaked open.

"Hello, Prefect." It was a woman I recognized from Friday. She was one of the women in the group accompanying the Nazarene. I was surprised she would even open the door.

"Hello, I am so sorry to bother you. It is my son's birthday, and he was hoping to see…, I'm sorry. I really didn't think anyone occupied this home. I would never have knocked. We are going now," I bowed my head slightly to her.

I can't play along with my son's fantasy.

"No, that's fine. I understand. My son was young once too, and often saw beyond our adult awareness."

"Your son?"

"Yeshua of Nazareth."

"Excuse my intrusion…"

"Pilo," Yeshua's mother stepped around me. "Pilo, my son and I wish you a Happy Birthday." Pilo leaned forward as she offered him a kiss.

"Thank you," I said to her. "I don't know your name."

"Myriam of Nazareth"

"Myriam," I lowered my voice, "I should tell you, we are looking for his body. I know you will want it back for proper burial."

"Mother of Yeshua, will you give him this robe. My Tata bought it for him," Pilo said as he handed Myriam the robe.

"I certainly will, Pilo. Thank you, Prefect."

"Ah…, you are welcome." Now, I was confused.

After that rather pleasant exchange, I mounted my horse. I looked at her for a moment. Myriam of Nazareth smiled at me and swayed a bit. *She's not telling me something.* She gave no indication that she was a grieving mother. Her eyes sparkled. She waved as we left.

Strange. The discomfort in the pit of my stomach had returned.

***

My disciples cowered in the far corner of the room, terrified that Pilate himself was coming after them.

"Lord, help us. What are we to do?"

My friends couldn't believe that I would send my mother to speak to Pontius Pilate. I laughed and watched out the shuttered window. The soldiers eyed my mother and the door. While Mother engaged Pilate in conversation, young Pilo scanned the building. I opened one of the slats in the shutter. Pilo could see me. I gave him a wink and the shish sign. He smiled and gave me a slight nod.

Pilo and his mother Claudia knew what my Father had revealed to them. Pilate had heard only lies. He would soon hear the truth.

31. I Was Not Sleeping

"SLEEPING? I SENT YOU AND THREE OTHER SOLDIERS to do the simple task of guarding a tomb, and you fall asleep! Do you have any idea what such dereliction of duty can cost you?"

Centurion Gaius Marius stood in front of my desk. He was silent, and looked straight ahead, as I outlined the possible punishment he could receive because of his actions.

"You could be discharged from the army and stripped of your rank. I could even have you flogged. How does that sound?" He shifted in place at that news.

"What do you have to say for yourself, soldier?" I demanded.

"I was not sleeping on duty, sir. The body of Yeshua of Nazareth was not stolen, sir. In my presence, and I was fully awake, the ground shook causing the stone covering the entrance to the tomb to roll away. That is when the three other soldiers left the area in fear. I stayed to see what was happening."

"A brilliant light emanated from the tomb. A man came out of the tomb and approached me. I fell to the ground in fear, until the man spoke to me, identified himself as Yeshua of Nazareth, and told me not to be afraid. He let me touch him so I could feel he was not a ghost. Yeshua of Nazareth is alive, sir; he has risen from the dead."

"Soldier, stop this nonsense immediately!"

"I beg your indulgence, sir, but I must continue."

"How dare you…"

"Yeshua told me to return to the barracks and tell the authorities what I witnessed. I did so, sir. I told Commander Rufus. He gave the other soldiers and me some money and ordered us not to speak of what we had witnessed, but to tell everyone that his followers stole his body. However, I cannot do that for that is not the truth. I have come to tell you the truth so that you too will know that he has risen. He sent me to inform you, and I have done so, sir."

I was astounded at the centurion's audacity, telling me such fantasies. It was bad enough for Yeshua's followers to be running around the city suggesting such nonsense, but for a Roman soldier, this was the punishable offense of giving false witness.

"How dare you speak to me with these lies. And you call yourself a soldier." I slammed my fist on the desk. I paced the floor pondering what to do with this man. He was Herod's soldier. I had to step carefully. I decided to let the Galilee Sepphoris district deal with him.

"I will inform your commander at the Sepphoris garrison of your negligence. You will leave with your contingent tomorrow. Now, get back to the barracks! You are relieved of duty in Jerusalem."

"Yes, sir," he said. "I would like to return the money Commander Rufus gave me. I cannot keep it."

I took the sack of money from his hand. "You are dismissed, soldier."

Curious as to why Commander Rufus would even try to buy the soldiers' silence, I shook the money out of the sack and counted it. "What? There's six months' worth of wages here."

I walked out onto the balcony and watched as the centurion headed back to the barracks. I rolled the sack of money around in my hand.

What's going on? Why would Rufus give them so much money to change their story?

I had a few questions for Commander Rufus.

32. Conspiracy

Tuesday morning

"PONTIUS, IT'S TIME TO GET UP. Commander Rufus is in your office. He needs to speak to you." Claudia's voice stirred me from a deep dreamless sleep. I was late.

I threw some water on my face, skipped breakfast and the prayer room. Duty called me to the Praetorium.

"What is it, Commander?" I asked him as I sat at my desk.

"Caiaphas has requested a meeting with you before you leave for Caesarea. There is the little matter of the dead man's followers spreading the word around that he has risen from the dead, and it is not sitting well with the High Priest," Commander Rufus told me.

"I just bet it isn't. What does he expect me to do about it?"

"He is outside, waiting for you, sir."

"Show him in."

"Yes, sir."

The High Priest, President of the Sanhedrin, Yosef Caiaphas, marched into my office and planted himself in front of my desk.

I rocked back in my chair. "Good morning, Yosef, what can I do for you today? Do you have somebody else you want me to crucify?"

"No, Prefect, I do not. And I don't appreciate that tone of voice."

"My tone of voice? Just who do you think is in charge here?"

Caiaphas stomped his foot on the floor. He pursed his mouth and huffed at me.

I'm going to play with him for a while before I kick him out of my office. I got up from my desk and stood squarely in front of him.

"What do you want, Yosef?"

"The followers of Yeshua of Nazareth, who you dispatched before Passover, are stirring up the people into believing that he has risen from the dead. This is intolerable."

"Have I not made myself clear to you? I don't care about your internal religious squabbles. Now get out of here. Deal with them yourself, isn't that the job of the Sanhedrin?"

"We need soldiers to rout them out of hiding. We don't have enough temple guards to do the task. We have no idea where these people are."

Funny, I know where they are. They are just a stone's throw from the Temple.

"The army is here to keep the peace and at this moment, I don't see any trouble. Jerusalem is peaceful and will be even more peaceful when... you... leave... my... office. The answer is no. Get out!"

The High Priest stomped out of the Practorium.

He will probably write another letter to Tiberius complaining about me. Frankly, I don't care if he does. I've got a mind to dismiss him.

Presently, I have an issue that demands an explanation from my Commander. I intend to find out exactly what happen on Sunday morning.

I walked to the entrance of the Praetorium where Caiaphas had just exited. I turned and walked back to my desk. I picked up the sack full of coins and tossed it in the air. I caught it and put it back on the desk.

"Commander Rufus, do you recognized this sack of coins?"

"No, sir."

Hmm.

"Centurion Gaius Marius from the Galilee district was in my office yesterday, and I confronted him about his dereliction of duty in failing to sufficiently guard the tomb of Yeshua of Nazareth."

"Yes, sir."

"He gave me this sack of coins. He said you gave him the money for his silence on what he had witnessed at the tomb. Also, he said, you ordered him to change his story, saying instead that Yeshua's body had been stolen."

"Do you have an explanation for this"?

Rufus was silent.

"What I want to know is this, who is telling me the truth, the centurion, or you?"

Rufus shifted his stance. His face turned red. He looked at the floor and then at the ceiling, anywhere but at me. That is not the behavior of a person about to tell me the truth.

"Marcus I'm waiting. One of you is lying. One of you needs to lose his head. Is it you or the centurion?"

I waited for a response.

"Do I have to repeat my question, Commander?"

Rufus swallowed hard.

"Sir, I did not give the soldiers any money. I did not tell them to change their explanation as to what happened at the tomb."

"Let me remind you, so that you understand, lying to the Emperor's provincial representative is punishable by death."

"Tell me what exactly happened on Sunday morning. I want the truth!"

"Yes, sir. Perhaps I should start with what I witnessed on Friday."

"Fine, go ahead."

"On Friday, on the way to Golgotha, the centurion gave the prisoner, Yeshua of Nazareth, frequent assistance. He gave him water several times. He enlisted someone to carry the crossbeam for him to Golgotha.

"The centurion is from Galilee, from the same area as the condemned man. I believe they were acquaintances, possibly even friends, sir. The centurion turned the responsibility for crucifying the Nazarene over to the other soldiers; he could not or would not do it himself. I had to order him to assure the man was dead. The centurion did spear the Nazarene through to his heart, but that was after he was dead. I heard the centurion call the Nazarene 'the Son of God,' meaning the Jews' God. The centurion showed deference to the man's family, sir. Later, I was told, he even assisted Yosef of Arimathea with the burial."

"Go on."

"Sir, I believe that the centurion helped the followers of Yeshua of Nazareth to remove the body from the grave. The sack you showed me is probably the money they gave him for helping them."

He could be telling me the truth. My head is pounding.

"Marcus, you have been the Commander of the forces here in Judea since my predecessor, Valerius Gratus, appointed you. I kept you on because he assured me you were a consummate Roman soldier, totally committed to the empire."

"What you have told me sounds like a reasonable and probable explanation. I have one question, though, was Yeshua of Nazareth actually dead?"

"Absolutely, sir."

"So, it's not possible that he regained consciousness in the tomb?" I could see the commander's shoulders relax as a smile crossed his face.

"Absolutely not, sir. He was as dead as I've seen anyone."

I paused to collect my thoughts.

"Commander Rufus, I will write a letter to the centurion's commander, advising him of Gaius Marius' dereliction of duty. You must provide me with a written account of what you witnessed. I will need you to come up with actual proof that he aided Yeshua's followers with the theft of his body. I can't recommend additional charges on speculation, regardless of how reasonable they seem."

"Sir."

"You are not to discuss this with anyone. Do you understand?"

"Yes, sir."

"You are dismissed, Commander."

He made a hasty exit.

My weariness of Jerusalem was growing.

**

I tried to catch up on the work still on my desk. I had to get the taxes done before we could head back to Caesarea. It was quiet, but as I worked, the noise from the scourging on Friday echoed in my head. I looked over at the blood stains on the floor leading out to the balcony. The Nazarene couldn't have survived the crucifixion. The stories both soldiers had given me just didn't add up. Then, there was the not-so-grieving-mother I met on Monday. I remembered my dream from the night before. I wanted to see the tomb of Yeshua of Nazareth for myself. I called for Cornelius.

My private security guard had become a friend. He was one of the few voices in Judea whose advice I could trust. I realized this after I ignored his warnings to me about hanging the banners bearing the image of the emperor in Jerusalem. I nearly had a riot on my hands during my first months in this province. Cornelius understood the Jews far better than anyone; I hoped he could figure out what happened on Sunday at the tomb of Yeshua of Nazareth.

"Cornelius, do you know where that Nazarene was buried?" I asked him before he was even in my office.

"I've heard it was in the burial garden not far from Golgotha. It is a walled garden where the wealthier Jews bury their dead."

"I've been told it was a tomb hued out for Yosef of Arimathea."

"Yes, sir."

"Can you take me there?"

"Yes, but the Jews might consider it an intrusion of their sacred place of the dead."

"Have you not heard the story of the possible resurrection of Yeshua of Nazareth going around?"

"Centurion Marius told me what happened when he was guarding the tomb."

"Do you believe him?"

"Ah, well, I don't know, sir. I've known Gaius Marius for some time. He has been coming to Jerusalem from Galilee with Herod for years. He seems to be an honest man. I wouldn't expect that he would make up a story about someone rising from the dead."

"I want to see the tomb myself. If the body has been stolen, we need to find evidence as that is a crime. If the centurion is telling the truth. Well, who knows what will happen."

"Yes, sir. I will have our steeds brought out."

***

The Garden of Tombs outside the Walls of Jerusalem

Cornelius suggested that we dismount before entering the Garden of Tombs so that the Jews would think we were showing respect for their dead. I followed his recommendation, not that I cared about the dead Jews. I just wanted to make sure one Jew, in particular, was still dead.

The garden was large and surrounded by a hillside of rock. The occupied tombs were covered by large carved out round stones. There were some trees scattered between the tombs. A few of the tombs were opened with their associated cover stones off to the side.

"How can we tell which one was the Nazarene's?" I asked.

"I'm sure it is the one with the stone flat on the ground over there," Cornelius said, as he pointed to the open tomb at the furthest end of the garden.

When we got to the site, I could see the ropes and wax seal on the stone. "Looks like you are correct, Cornelius. Shall we have a look inside?"

"It will be dark, sir. It will take a bit for our eyes to adjust."

I admit, I was apprehensive about entering the tomb, especially after the dream I had had. I motioned to Cornelius to go first.

"Let me know what you find," I said.

I waited for his assessment.

"You might want to come in, sir."

"Fine."

I ducked through the narrow opening. "I can't see anything. It's too dark."

"Let your eyes adjust, sir."

They did. I could see the interior of the tomb quite well. The burial shroud was on a narrow rock shelf folded in half with three sets of bindings still tied but laying loose around it. The cloth was shaped as though it still held a body. There were areas on it near the fold which were soaked with blood and again at the other end where the feet would have been. Mid-way down was a large flowing spot on the side of the shroud. *The spear wound*, I thought. There was blood on the front of the shroud where the hands rested.

There was another smaller cloth folded up by itself near the head of the shroud.

I felt shivers down my back. The scene was exactly as it was when I dreamed of the Nazarene showing me his tomb. I stepped back and put my hand on the wall to steady myself.

"Are you alright, sir? Cornelius asked.

"Yes, yes, I'm... I'm fine. What do you think Cornelius? It doesn't seem like it was even touched by thieves."

"No, sir, it doesn't.

"Bring the shroud. We can't leave it here as evidence."

"Yes, sir. What will we do with it?"

"Take it back to Caesarea with us. See that it is destroyed."

"Yes, sir."

33. Emmaus

W E DEPARTED JERUSALEM AFTER LUNCH. Tax complaints delayed our departure until the afternoon. Our route would take us to Arimathea before sundown where we planned to spend the night.

To make up for lost travel time, the carriage driver pressed the team of two horses. The carriage rattled against the paving stones. I feared the passengers would get upset with being shaken so much. Claudia was already annoyed with our late departure. Claudia's servant, Sarah, a Jew, was in the carriage with her.

"Pontius, must we go so fast. My bones are hurting," Claudia called out the window.

I led the contingent on my steed. Even he couldn't wait to get home, it was all I could do to keep him from breaking into a gallop. I reined one-handed as Pilo sat in front of me. I had one hand around his waist. We were going faster than we did on the brief tour around Jerusalem. He had a broad grin on his face.

"Faster, Tata, faster," he said.

Pilo had become a constant reminder to me of the Nazarene. I couldn't shake the discomfort I felt over his death. When I left Jerusalem, the soldiers still hadn't found his body.

It was a relief leaving the city. I have more than my share of problems every time I go there. This trip was no exception. I didn't expect to be back to Jerusalem until the Jews' next feast which was Shavuot. It was much less provocative than Passover. The Jews happily celebrate their first harvest, and I collect taxes.

I consciously scanned the hillsides and surrounding area. I did let Barabbas go, so I was concerned that he could soon start a murderous rampage against us. Our own spies had no idea of his whereabouts. Our guards formed a tight protection net around us. They too were aware that Barabbas was on the loose.

Why did I let him go?

I had no idea how I was going to explain my judgment to the Emperor. Information about my actions seemed to have a way of getting back to Tiberius, even without me telling him.

Cornelius rode next to me. He had the shroud wrapped in a blanket and strapped to the back of a pack horse. I knew what it was, but no one else did.

The road was full of pilgrims leaving Jerusalem. Claudia warned me not to push people off the road. I think their curses bothered her. The crowd slowed our progress, but it gave me a chance to people watch, which was not something I normally did. What I saw in the travelers' faces was a combination of fear and derision. I believe that if people feared us Romans, it would keep them from causing trouble.

I laughed as Pilo waved to people from his position on my steed. Some of them waved back at him. One father pulled his child's hand down as he tried to return Pilo's wave.

A sudden clatter and Claudia's scream from behind shook me out of my private thoughts.

"Whoa…" One of the soldiers hollered at the carriage driver.

I turned about and saw that the back end of the carriage was leaning to the right. A wheel had come off.

"What's going on?" I demanded to know. "Claudia, are you injured?"

"No, but will somebody help me out," she called.

Her servant girl climbed out the high side of the carriage. A couple of soldiers lifted the fallen side. Claudia clambered out and brushed herself off.

"Well, that won't do. The wheel is off. Now, what do we do?"

"Can it be repaired?" I asked the men.

"The axle is broken, sir. It has split. We will have to find a skilled laborer to fix it."

"Where do we find such a person out here? Jerusalem is seven miles back that way."

"Actually, the town Emmaus, just ahead of us, sir, has skilled men who live there. They make a significant income repairing carts and carriages. It will probably take them a few hours to fix it, sir," the carriage driver reported.

"If that is the case, we won't make Arimathea before sundown."

"There is a favorable roadside inn at Emmaus, sir. I know they serve good food and have clean rooms. It's that place up the road from here," he said pointing to a large two-story building.

"Fine, we'll go there."

"Claudia, grab my arm, I'll pull you on behind me."

"I will not. How do you expect me to sit on the beast?"

I got her point. Her clothing would not allow her to ride comfortably on the steed's back. "Do you think you can walk to that inn up ahead?"

"If you walk with me," she whimpered, as she looked up at me from the corner of her eyes.

I dismounted. Pilo slipped back in the saddle. He sat tall, he liked having the horse to himself. "Hang on Pilo."

"I will Tata."

I held the reins and walked arm-in-arm with Claudia. We both laughed. I suddenly wished there were no soldiers around us and that we were walking on the beach in Caesarea. The Emmaus Inn was a few yards away. It was a pleasant walk. I noticed that the road was in need of some repair work. The well-traveled road had missing and chipped stones. It would take a few hundred Sestertii to replace the stones just in this section alone.

No wonder there is a prosperous cart repair business in the small town. I should collect more taxes from them.

The innkeeper was surprised to see the Prefect of Judea entering his establishment. By his open mouth, it was hard to tell if he was afraid or pleased.

"Have you got a room for a family of three and a few soldiers for the night?" I asked him in my best Greek, which is the language of most merchants. I hadn't picked up the street language of Aramaic, yet. I could get by in Hebrew, but I saved that for Caiaphas and the priests.

"Yes, we certainly have, Prefect. We have a large room, which would probably suit your needs. We usually put the soldiers up in the long room in the back."

"We also have two servants, who are husband and wife."

"We have room, sir."

"I've been told you have good meals here. When do you start serving?"

"At sundown, sir. The dining room is off to your left."

The innkeeper took us up a set of creaky stairs and showed us to our room on the second floor. The spacious room had a double window, which looked out on the road. There was one large bed, which could hold the three of us comfortably. Claudia flopped on it.

"How long do you suppose the repair will take?" she asked.

"It will probably be ready tomorrow morning; at least, I hope it will."

"Do you think we can go a little slower tomorrow? My bones are still shaking from that ride, and we are barely out of Jerusalem," Claudia complained.

"You can soak in the pool when we get home," I told her.

"I suppose, by late afternoon it will be warm enough," she sighed.

I threw my satchel on the small desk in the corner by the window. I took my scabbard off and put it next to the satchel. Pilo leaned his chin on the window ledge and peered out at the passing travelers.

There was a knock on the door. Our servant had our baggage. "I didn't want to leave them in the carriage, sir. Someone might help themselves if you know what I mean."

"Very responsible of you Leo, thank you."

I glanced at the bags. I had one, Claudia had five, and we were only in Jerusalem a few days. She saw me looking at them. "I must have the same comforts in Jerusalem as I do in Caesarea."

"I didn't say anything."

"You were thinking it."

"Women."

"Men."

Pilo turned around and laughed at us.

Claudia reached out for Pilo, "Come, Pilo, you and mommi can have a nap."

"What's Tata going to do?" he asked.

"Work."

"You always work, Tata."

"I have to write a letter to the Emperor."

I pulled a chair up to the desk. I took a scroll and stylus out of my satchel and wrote.

Greetings, most August Divine Tiberius Caesar, from Pontius Pilatus,

I trust you are in good health, for which we give thanks to the gods.

I am pleased to report the peaceful observance of the Jewish Feast of Passover. There were no uprisings or conflicts. Before the feast, I found three men guilty of capital offenses. Two were murderers and thieves. In attempting to steal horses from the Jerusalem barracks, they killed a soldier. They did not request a hearing. No trial was necessary as Commander Marcus Rufus gave a written witness to the charges.

The Sanhedrin President, Yosef Caiaphas, brought a man before me for sentencing. The charge the Sanhedrin had against him was sedition. They declared him a threat to the Pax Romana, as he proclaimed himself 'King of the Jews,' a direct affront to your majesty. He gave no defense, nor did he seek the assistance of a defense solicitor.

These men were sentenced to death by crucifixion:

Dysmas, a Syrian Jew, 29 yrs. – Murder and Stealing Roman property

Gestas, a Syrian Jew, 30 yrs. – Murder and Stealing Roman property

Iesus, a Galilean Jew, 33 yrs. - Sedition

I enclosed the Edicts of Crucifixion appropriately signed and sealed.

In your service and the service of the Empire,

Pontius Pilatus, Praefectus Iudea.

There it is done. I hope he does not ask for a full account of the Galilean's trial.

***

Supper hour arrived, and I have to admit I hated the thought of not having a private room for eating. We would have to dine in the same place as the Jews and other wayfarers. Claudia, however, was excited as we approached the dining room. She likes people, no matter what class they are. She married me.

The dining room was a good size. The tables were staggered so that they didn't butt up against each other. The innkeeper's wife showed us to a table at the front of the room. It was in a private corner next to the window. The shutters were open. Claudia and Pilo sat facing the window. I faced the interior of the dining room.

Cornelius joined us and sat across from me. "This is not a secure building, sir. I will be nearby in case of trouble."

"Of course, Cornelius," I replied.

A lamp burned in the middle of the table. There was a generous plate of grapes, figs, and pomegranates. We rarely ate in a public place, so this was an uncommon dining experience for us. I glanced around at the other patrons. Some glared at me.

The innkeeper's wife brought us a bowl of water and towels. It was a Jewish custom to wash their hands before eating. I washed my hands and passed the bowl to Claudia. Our hostess cleared her throat.

I looked at her. "Yes?"

"You are expected to wash up to your elbows, Prefect."

"Oh, yes, I forgot," ...*another one of those Jewish rules. I don't know how they keep track of them*. I obliged her. *Next time we are getting a private dining room.*

"Wine or ale for you, sir?" she asked.

"Ale for me, wine for my wife, and a grape drink for my son," I replied.

Claudia frowned at me, but in an establishment like this, ale seemed the most appropriate drink for a man.

Within a few minutes, we had our drinks served, followed immediately by bowls of steaming lamb stew along with a basket of hot corn bread. It all smelled good.

Activity outside caught Pilo's attention, his eyes followed something. I turned around to look, but I didn't see anything unusual, just a man lighting the torches at the front of the inn.

"What were you looking at Pilo?" I asked him.

"I thought I recognized somebody, Tata," he said. "But, I'm not sure."

"Who?"

"I couldn't see him very well."

"Finish your stew."

The room filled quickly. The noise level went up too. Three men took the table behind ours. Two of the men had their backs to me. The third man faced me. His head covering obscured his face. It occurred to me that his white robe looks similar to the one I bought in the market, and Pilo gave to the Nazarene's mother.

We continued to enjoy our meal. My driver was right the food was good. I thought about having seconds. I watched as Pilo soaked up the stew with the bread. He punched it down into the stew with the spoon. Then threw his head back and dumped a spoon full of the mess into his mouth. The sauced dripped down both sides of his grinning mouth.

"Pilo, don't play with your food," Claudia told him. We both laughed.

As I reached for my ale, the man opposite me took his head covering down. I glimpsed his smiling face. The noise from my mug smashing to the table and hitting the bowl of stew startled everyone in the room. The room went silent.

"Pontius, what's wrong?" Claudia asked.

I quickly regained my composure and grabbed the mug, too late; most of its contents were on the table, or in the bowl of stew. I glanced up again. The man I saw was gone. The other two men were excitedly talking to each other. They got up and departed the dining room.

The rest of the patrons clapped at my mug dropping performance.

Claudia followed my line of sight. "What did you see, Pontius?" she whispered. "You're pale. Are you ill?"

"I'm… I'm fine."

The innkeeper's wife was at our table cleaning up the mess I made. "Would you like more, sir?"

"Yes, please, I'm sorry about this..."

"More stew too?"

"Certainly."

Claudia and Pilo continued to stare at me. I was aware that I was shaking. They could probably see it. My hands trembled. I put them down to my side and took a deep breath. I nodded to Claudia. She creased her brow but didn't say anything.

I looked over at Cornelius, who was staring at me. I didn't know what to say to him. He leaned across the gap between us.

"I saw him too sir. He just disappeared."

I nodded. I was relieved that I was not hallucinating.

We finished our meal in silence. This old soldier has faced enemies in battle. That evening, I was shaken by the appearance of a dead man, Yeshua of Nazareth.

I stared out the window at nothing in particular. Claudia came up behind me, wrapped her arms around my waist, and leaned her head against my back.

"Pontius, what happened at supper tonight?" she asked.

I glanced over my shoulder at Pilo, sleeping soundly on the bed. The amber glow from the single lamp on the desk lit his face. I had to tell her something believable. I decided to tell her the truth.

"I saw him, Claudia."

"Who dear?"

"Yeshua of Nazareth. He was at the table behind you. His hood obscured his face, at first, then he took it off. He nodded at me and smiled. It was him, of that, I have no doubt. Cornelius also saw him." I turned to face her. She looked up at me with a broad smile on her face; tears formed in her eyes.

"Pontius, that's wonderful. I'm so glad. I haven't seen him myself. Joanna has. She and a couple of other women went to his grave early Sunday morning. Beings appeared to them and told them that Yeshua had risen. Joanna saw him later when he appeared to his followers that evening."

"You seemed to know something early Sunday morning."

"A Being of Light told me that the man I sought to save from crucifixion had risen from the dead. At first, I thought it was a dream, but the Being assured me I wasn't dreaming. He also told me to forgive you, my husband, for God has used your weakness to bring about salvation for all. That's why I'm not angry with you anymore."

"I see. And Pilo? What does he know?"

"Ask him in the morning. He is just dying to tell you. He was advised to wait."

"By you?"

"No."

"Beings?"

"No."

"The Nazarene?"

"Yes."

I pulled Claudia closer to me.

…Hmm, it's been way too long since I've felt her kiss.

We crawled into bed on either side of Pilo. I felt at peace for the first time since I sent the Nazarene to the cross.

34. Fishers of Men

On the Shore of the Sea of Galilee

Thursday, Near Sunrise

I TOLD MY FRIENDS I WOULD MEET with them in Galilee. Peter, Andrew, James, and John were back to catching fish, not exactly the fish I had in mind for them. The non-fishermen were in the boat with them.

Simon Peter's boat was just off shore. It wasn't a good night for fishing. Their nets were empty. Even from the beach, I could see their long faces. They looked lost. I needed to remind them of their mission. I have called them to be fishers of men.

It was time to call Simon Peter back into friendship with me. I needed my Rock.

Before I invited them ashore, I had to get a fire going and convince some fish to come for breakfast.

It had been a while since I started a fire from scratch. I found two sticks and some dry grass. I rubbed the sticks together fast. There was a smolder. I rubbed them faster. There was a little spark. *My mission will start with a spark in the hearts of those I have called.* As I blew gently on the burning embers, the fire grew. *I will fan the Fire of Faith with the Holy Spirit.*

I built up the fire with more wood. I placed a large rock in the fire, on which to cook the fish. *On my Rock, I will build my church.* It was time to call them, again.

"My friends, have you caught anything."

"No."

"Cast your nets on the other side."

They pulled their nets up and cast them to the other side of the boat. Immediately, their net was near breaking with fish. John recognized me. "It is the Lord," he shouted.

They were not that far out. Peter threw off his cloak and jumped into the water naked. I laughed as he staggered up the beach to me. The others rowed ashore, got out of the boat and dragged the net up the beach.

"Bring some of the fish you caught and we'll have breakfast," I told them.

Wide-eyed they were still not used to seeing me. I visited them, but I did not remain with them for very long. They were leaderless. They needed their gentle helmsman.

We sat in a circle around the fire. James added more fish to the few that I had cooking on the rock. They were nervous. Simon Peter sat directly across from me. He took only brief glances at me, still not making eye contact.

It was time for a reconciliation.

"Simon bar Jonah, do you love me more than these?"

Peter looked at me and then looked away. The others were silent.

"Yes, Lord, you know I love you," he whispered.

"Feed my lambs."

He shuffled in his place. He briefly made eye contact with me.

"Simon bar Jonah, do you love me?"

Peter put his piece of fish down and rubbed his mouth on his sleeve. This time, I held his eyes to mine for a few seconds.

"Yes, Lord, you know I love you."

"Take care of my sheep."

Peter was getting antsy; he did not like me focusing on him.

"Simon bar Jonah, do you love me?"

I touched his heart. The tears poured down his face. He stood, walked over, and knelt in front of me.

"Lord, you know all things. You know I love you," he sobbed.

With my hand on his shoulder, I told him, "Take care of my sheep."

We embraced. He accepted my forgiveness. My Rock had come home, and he would be a source of strength for his brothers and sisters.

I invited Peter to walk with me on the beach. John followed at a short distance.

"I tell you, Peter, when you were young you put on your own belt and went where you wanted to go. When you are old you will stretch out your hands and somebody else will put a belt on you and you will go where you would rather not. You will follow me."

Peter glanced back at John. "And what is to become of him?"

"If I want him to stay until I come, what is that to you? You are to follow me."

***

I gathered them all together and led them up the shore. I continued to speak to them about the future. I told them it would not be easy; they will suffer much for my sake.

We spent the day together. I took them around the lake to the spot, which overlooks the Sea of Galilee where I addressed the crowd of five thousand. I reminded my apostles about that day.

"Can you recall the teaching I gave you on this hillside?"

"Blessed are the poor?" John replied

The others shook their heads. I glanced at Peter. He was still nervous. I smiled and waved to encourage him. He had something on the tip of his tongue.

"What father among you would hand your child a stone if he asked for bread? So too will your Father in heaven give good things to those who ask him," he blurted out. Peter beamed with pride that he remembered something. Yes, that is something a family man would remember.

They tried… their memories were weak.

"It was three years ago, Master," Matthew said. "How can we possibly remember everything you said that day?"

"I remember how you fed everyone with the few loaves and fishes," Andrew added.

Yes, they remember the miracles.

Philip stood. "I remember the words you gave us to say when we pray."

"Yes, Philip, speak from your heart," I told him. Everyone went quiet. I could hear the wind rustling the grass.

"Our Father, who is in heaven…"

The others remembered too. They joined him. I laid back against a tree and closed my eyes. It was the first time my disciples had prayed together the words I gave them. My heart brimmed with joy, tears formed in my eyes. The Holy Spirit will help them remember everything I taught them. It is because of their words that many will come to believe in me. I had a vision in my heart. People all over the world are praying to the Father in the words I taught these disciples. My mission was in their hands.

***

We sat on the grass and had a meal together. The sun was low in the western sky. They were quiet, reflecting on this moment.

John leaned over to me, put his hand on mine and whispered, "Master, please stay with us."

"I must return to the Father so that the Spirit will come."

John lowered his eyes. He did not understand why I should leave them a second time.

As evening neared, I told them to go back to Jerusalem, and I would see them there. One of my friends was a holdout. He did not believe the story of my resurrection that the others have told him. He needed to see me and to touch me.

I will leave no one behind in doubt.

35. The Truth

Emmaus

Thursday Morning

"I'LL BE OUT IN A FEW MINUTES, dear, I must get ready," Claudia called from the second-floor window.

Why is it that a woman must always 'get ready'? What is there to do but get dressed?

Pilo and I waited outside the inn by my steed. I gave him the groomers' brush. He loved to groom my horse. He stood on his own. I used to have to hold him. I felt grateful for his healing.

Two soldiers stood a few feet away on the other side of my horse. They were conversing. I could hear them.

"I can't stop thinking about Sunday morning at that tomb we were guarding."

"Neither can I."

"I heard the centurion actually went to Pilate and told him what really happened."

"Yes, and it is not looking good for him. He could get severely punished for negligence."

"I can't believe that Commander Rufus paid us to lie, you know, change our story. I mean, he was there. He saw what happened."

"Pilate would probably come down hard on him and all of us, if he knew. We were supposed to prevent that man's body from being stolen or disappearing."

"I don't know how it happened. I mean, a flash of light and the man just walked out of the tomb on his own. I've never known of anyone walking away from being crucified. It's all very strange."

"Did you see Centurion Marius on his knees in the middle of that white light?"

"No, I was watching Commander Rufus hiding in the trees. He was shaking like a leaf when he got back to the barracks."

"Centurion Marius wasn't though. He stood there in front of the Commander announcing, without an ounce of trepidation, that Yeshua of Nazareth had risen from the dead."

"I heard Pilate gave orders we were to look for the body."

"Yes, I'm sure we…"

"I'm ready to go now. Haven't you got the horse prepared yet?" Claudia's voice came from behind me. The soldiers' voices faded

"Ah, yes, well, Pilo was just doing a bit of grooming."

I tightened the straps of the saddle a bit harder than I should. *Commander Rufus lied to me…he'll be digging his own grave.*

"Tata, are you going to lift me so I can get on the horse?" Pilo's words broke my thoughts.

"Yes, put your foot here." I cupped my hands and lifted him onto the steed's back at the front of the saddle and mounted the horse behind him. I dared not look at the soldiers. I did not want them to know I heard them.

Claudia and her servant girl settled in the carriage. I checked the repair job. It seemed secure enough.

"Let's move out," I ordered.

"Sir, the men who repaired the axle have advised me that we should go easy on our way back to Caesarea because the other axles are in poor condition," my driver said.

"How easy?"

"Just a little over walking speed."

"What?"

"Yes, sir. We will probably have to stop again, sir."

"Fine then, let's get moving. When we do manage to get back to Caesarea, I want the carriage checked thoroughly for problems. Do I make myself clear?"

"Yes, sir."

Delays are unacceptable. We would have to stop in Arimathea and Lydda.

***

The road wasn't crowded. The stopover put us behind the masses leaving Jerusalem. I rode beside Claudia's carriage, after the mishap, I felt it was best to be near her.

Pilo was positioned on the steed in front of me, presenting an excellent opportunity for me to have a chat with him.

"Pilo, do you know what happened to me at supper last night?"

"You dropped your ale, Tata."

"Do you know why?"

Pilo turned around and gave me a quizzical look. "Why Tata?"

"I saw the Nazarene. He was sitting at the table behind you."

"Tata! You did? You saw Yeshua!" Pilo bellowed.

"Shish, Pilo. We don't want everyone to know."

Pilo hunched down. I glanced around; some of the soldiers were staring at me. The two soldiers who had been at Yeshua's grave stopped their horses in their tracks. They heard him.

"Pilo, I want you to keep this to yourself. We don't want to confuse people who think he is dead."

"Yes, Tata. I saw him too. At the house in Jerusalem, when you were speaking with his mother. Yeshua was looking from the shuttered window above us."

"Was he now?"

"He gave me the sign not to tell. So I didn't. Tata, don't be mad at me," Pilo pleaded.

"No, Pilo. I'm not mad at you. I understand."

"Are you angry at the Commander for not telling you?"

It occurred to me that Pilo heard the conversation between the soldiers.

"The Commander needs to tell me the truth when things happen. It is his job. You should tell me the truth too, but sometimes it is alright to wait. You didn't lie to me. There is a difference."

"Are you going to hurt the Commander? Yeshua wouldn't like that."

"Well, I don't know." My son was getting to be more like his mother. "It is important to keep the rules in the army. Otherwise, we might not be able to keep things orderly and peaceful."

"Yes, Tata."

I glanced back at the two soldiers who had caught up with us. They were riding closer to me. I suspected they wanted to talk. I motioned them forward.

"I heard you two speaking back at Emmaus."

They looked at me wide-eyed.

"Yes, sir," one of them said.

"I want you both to go back to Jerusalem and tell Commander Rufus that I want to see him in Caesarea immediately."

"Yes, sir."

"You can keep the money he gave you," I told them. That put a smile on their faces.

I need to find a new commander.

36. James of Nazareth

JAMES AND I GREW UP TOGETHER. He is eighteen months older than I am. His mother died giving birth to him. That is why Yosef sought another wife and arranged with my grandfather, Joachim, to marry my mother. Yosef had five other children, but I was closest in age to James.

From an early age, I followed James everywhere. He was my brother, and I adored him. If he did something, I did the same thing. We were great friends, until one day when we were searching for firewood.

The small stand of trees at the edge of the forest on the upper side of Nazareth was familiar terrain to us. We played in there, practiced building houses out of branches, and even scraped our knees climbing a few trees. That day, in the spring of the year I turned nine, is one I will not forget. It happened so fast that I never thought twice about doing what I did.

James was running ahead of me trying to pick up more sticks than me. We were both laughing so much; we could hardly see where we were going. I stopped at one point to retrieve a large stick when I heard James scream. I dropped everything and ran over to him. He laid on the ground crying, wreathing, and holding his leg. Out of the corner of my eye, I saw a venomous snake slithering away. Something inside of me took over. I reached down and put my hands on James' leg, and prayed. The painful red wound cleared. I healed him.I was pleased.

James was suddenly terrified, of me! He immediately ran home, leaving me somewhat bewildered in the woods. When I finally got home, he was telling mother and father what I had done. James ran out of the room as I entered. In near tears, I called out to him, but he kept going. My parents took me aside. They assured me that I had done nothing wrong, but asked me to go and get help if anything like that ever happened again. It was best.

Not long after that, they sat me down and told me about my birth. Angels? Wise men? I was so confused if not a little frightened when they said that I was the Son of the Most High. I was not Yosef's natural son. However, Yosef assured me, that he loved me as his own. My parents advised me that I should tell no one about these things until I was much older. They said that my brothers and sisters did not know. That proved to be a problem later when I started my mission.

My family had heard about my preaching and healing of people. They thought I was ill, mad, or out of my mind. They begged me to come home. Mother was with them. She too was confused and worried about me. Mother's concern never relented. She was overprotective of me as a child, kissing every bruise and scrape I managed to collect while keeping up with James.

***

It had been too long; reconciliation with James was overdue. I needed him.

James was a devout man, he was the rabbi of Nazareth's synagogue, so I was not surprised that I should find him praying over the scriptures in his small prayer room at that early hour. The incense rose behind the small lamp he had set beside the scroll.

He was rocking back and forth as he brushed the tears from his face. "Adonai, Adonai. I am so grieved. My brother, my dear brother, dead at the hands of the Romans. Adonai, Adonai."

James had heard about my death. Even though he has not spoken to me in three years, he was a broken man. News of my resurrection had not reached Nazareth. Mother was in Capernaum with her sister and John.

I sat on a cushion behind James; I didn't want him to get another scare from me.

There is no easy way to do this.

He knelt back on his knees with his hands to his face. He was praying the morning psalms. I cleared my throat. He stopped praying. He knew he was not alone.

"Simon, is that you?" he said, thinking it was our older brother who lives with him.

"No, James, it's me, Yeshua. Peace be with you."

James dropped his hands to his side and slowly turned to face me. His eyes grew as large as grapes.

"Fear not, I am not a ghost," I said as I reached for him to touch me. We were only a couple of feet from each other. James did not get up; instead, he threw himself on me. I caught him in an embrace. "I love you, my brother."

James sobbed, "I thought you were dead!"

"I was."

"But how...? You are...are here!"

"I have risen."

James was speechless. He ran his hands over my wounds and wept. "Can you forgive my disbelief?"

"You are my brother... I have always loved you."

"I ran from you. I've been running from you all these years."

"Come back, James. That's all I've ever wanted you to do. Come back to me, for I am your brother in more ways than the flesh could ever make us brothers."

"Yeshua, Anna tried to tell me. It was after Yosef died. An old woman's tales I thought. If only I had listened."

We held each other for a few minutes. "I want you to go to Jerusalem, to the Upper Room, and wait for me. My disciples will be there. Bring the others, if they wish to come. Tell them they will see me."

James wiped the tears from his face and nodded.

"Shalom, my brother," I said as I squeezed his hand.

"Shalom."

37. Missive from Tiberius

Caesarea Maritima,

The Palace

Saturday

THE SCROLL FROM TIBERIUS was on the desk unopened in front of me. It was always unnerving when communication came unexpectedly from the Emperor himself. Unofficial channels indicated to me that the purge of Sejanus associates had not subsided. Was it my turn? Political fortunes can turn quickly. A few years after my appointment to Judea, Sejanus, who had been my promoter before the Emperor, plotted against Tiberius. The executions followed.

I stared at the scroll. The seal was genuine. I calmed my nerves with another mouth full of strong wine from Gallia. It was either one of two orders, commit suicide here or return to Rome for execution.

Pilo's laughter from outside distracted me. I strolled to the archway. He and Claudia were enjoying a late afternoon swim in the pool. What would happen to them if I was convicted of treason against the Emperor, if only through association?

I took the scroll in my hands and broke the seal. I could not see the words from the sweat that seeped into my eyes. A quick wipe cleared my vision. The words came into focus.

It was not what I feared. Tiberius appointed Lucius Vitellius as Legate of Syria. He would be my first report. The position had been vacant since I came to Judea. If there was an uprising and I needed additional soldiers, I must appeal to him. So, that was the answer to the petition for more soldiers I made a few months earlier.

I met Vitellius at social-political gatherings in Rome. I can't say that I particularly liked the man.

Perhaps, Tiberius appointed him to keep an eye on me. Whatever the reason, this could be my last chance to find favor with Tiberius. I must get myself invited to Syria as soon as possible.

Relieved that the scroll did not contain my fate, I continued to read. I put my feet up on the desk and relaxed.

"I've had a report of a Jewish healer from Galilee, who heals illnesses and malformed bodies. I've been told that he spends most of his time in your province."

My feet were back on the floor. I read on.

"I have need of a healer, especially a good one. The Roman and Greek physicians in my court have no healing skills. The report indicated that this Jewish healer can cure anything, including death itself.

Put him on the earliest transport to Rome. Pay him, if he so demands. I assure you of reimbursement. If he has returned to Galilee, send this request to Herod.

Greetings to my niece and her son

Tiberius Caesar, Emperor of Rome

Island of Capri"

"How did he learn of the Nazarene? Someone is giving Tiberius reports about my province," I said out loud. Fortunately, no one was in the room.

I need to find out who provided him with this information. He might hear that one of the men I ordered crucified was the Galilean he seeks.

I turned my thoughts back to the event at Emmaus. *Perhaps I can find Yeshua of Nazareth again. He may agree to visit the Emperor. I will have to contact his followers. Yosef of Arimathea might know where he is staying and could direct the Emperor's request to him.*

"Tata, Tata, come and watch me!" Pilo's voice echoed in the portico from the pool below. Still holding the scroll, I strolled down to poolside.

"What can you do, Pilo?" I asked.

"Mater has taught me how to swim. Watch, Tata, watch."

With that, my boy stretched out across the water's surface kicking his legs and feet as fast as he could. Sure enough, he swam. That Galilean healer came to mind again. I tucked the scroll under my arm, and I gave my son a hearty applause.

I glanced out at the sea, Mare Nostrum [Our Sea]. The distance between Judea and Italia was shrinking, most likely not to my benefit.

38. Thomas

THEY WERE IN THE UPPER ROOM waiting for me. Thomas was there. It was time for me to open his mind and heart to accepting the testimony of others.

"Shalom." Once again, I stood in their midst. Thomas stared at me and shook his head from side to side. I was there for him.

"Thomas, come and touch me. Know that I am not a ghost. See my hands and my side. Come, put your hand on the wound in my side, and believe."

Thomas took tentative steps in my direction. He glanced around at the others, who encouraged him to touch me. He moved a little closer and hesitated. Thomas reached out his hand; it hovered near my left arm. I took his hand in mine and move his fingers to the nail wound. Then I moved his hand to my side and slipped the end of his fingers into the spear wound.

Thomas dropped hard to his knees. "Adonai," he said at first. Then the words came from his heart, the words that echo through the ages. "My Lord and my God!"

He grasped my hand and wept. I caressed his head in my hands and held his face up to mine.

"You believe, Thomas because you have seen and touched me. How happy are those who have not seen and touched me and yet believe."

I knelt down to be at his level. I wrapped my arms around him. He embraced me. The tears poured down his face.

I love Thomas.

39. Called to Galilee

Caesarea Maritima

Sunday morning,

"I CAN'T EXPLAIN IT, PONTIUS, but I just have to go to Galilee today."

"You can try and explain why you are going there and taking our son with you. Is that too much to ask?"

"I know in my heart that we must go. Please, there's nothing more I can say."

"Fine, fine, but you are not going without protection. I will send Cornelius with you."

"Good. Now, will you order my carriage be readied?"

"I'm told they have completed the repairs to the other axles so it is safe. It is waiting for you."

"Good. See you in a few days…come Pilo."

Claudia gave me a peck on the cheek as they headed out the door.

Cornelius stood next to the carriage. He helped Claudia in as Pilo scampered in by himself. Cornelius gave me a salute and a wink. Pilo waved and kept waving as the carriage pulled out of sight.

Claudia and Pilo were off to Galilee. She insisted that she had to go, for reasons I could not fathom. I believed it was wise to send Cornelius with them. He was a tough soldier; no one could get by him and endanger my family.

40. Commander Rufus

Monday

IRECEIVED WORD YESTERDAY that Commander Marcus Rufus was on his way. It was about time. I sent those soldiers back to Jerusalem six days before with an order that he was to come to see me immediately. His delay was unacceptable.

The great thing about the palace was how Herod the Great built it. I had views of the entire landscape. I could see the sea plus all the roads that lead into Caesarea. Excellent planning.

One could always note the arrival of friends and, most importantly, the advance of an enemy. Out the south portico, I saw a single horse and rider meandering his way to the palace. Commander Rufus was not in a hurry.

I sat at my desk and waited.

"Commander Rufus to see you, sir," said my secretary, Alexander, a Greek-educated Jew.

Rufus marched into my office.

"Commander, I sent an order for you to come here immediately. Your delay is unacceptable."

"Sorry, sir, I was attending to the business of the remaining troops in Jerusalem."

"Your business is whatever I tell you it is. If I give an order for your immediate presence, I expect obedience!

"Yes, sir."

Rufus couldn't look at me. His eyes were fixed on the floor. He had no idea what was about to happen.

"Marcus, I am removing you as commander of the forces in Judea. You are to leave Judea immediately."

"Sir, I don't understand. What…What have I done." Rufus turned pale.

I walked around the desk and I planted myself directly in front of him.

"You lied to me. That is enough to warrant the death penalty. Fortunately for you, I'm in a lenient mood."

"But, Sir, I..I... did not…"

"Enough! What do you take me for, a fool? You saw exactly what happened at the tomb of the Nazarene because you were there. You paid the soldiers to lie. They didn't. Then, in front of me, you implicated the Galilean centurion of grave misconduct of his duties. Rufus, get out of Judea, now before I change my mind and dispatch you myself!"

Rufus had exited from my office before I got my last words out. My head was throbbing. I imbibed in the wine from Gallia. I needed more. It was getting low.

Cup in hand, I walked to the south portico. Rufus was mounting his steed. He rode north. That direction would take him to Galilee or possibly beyond to Syria. He would be out of my jurisdiction.

I need another Tribune. I drained my cup of wine.

41. All My Disciples

On the hillside by the Sea of Galilee

THE DAY OF MY RETURN TO THE FATHER was fast approaching. There were more people I wanted to see. Some men and women who counted themselves among my disciples were still in mourning because of my death. My angels have been hard at work encouraging them to gather on the hillside overlooking the Sea of Galilee. Many did not know why they were inexorably drawn to the place where I taught them. They came, called by an inner voice, speaking the angel's words, "He has risen."

I watched as they gathered around me. I greeted those who had come from near and far, as they did that day three years ago. They had all heard of my death. Some stood in silence before me.

"It is really him?" Some whispered.

"Peace be with you. Fear not, it is I," I said to them. I reached out to each person so they could touch me and feel that I was not a ghost.

My apostles were there, as were my family members from Nazareth. James had brought them. Lazarus, Yosef of Arimathea, and Nicodemus came from Jerusalem. Joanna, Lazarus' sisters Miriam and Martha, Mariam of Magdala, and Suzanna gathered with me, as they had since the beginning of my ministry. I embraced them all.

I looked out over the crowd of people, men, women, and children. Their eyes were fixed on me.

"Come to me all you who have sadness of heart and I will give you joy."

They moved a little bit closer to me. Their faces glowed.

"Love one another as I have loved you."

"Do unto others as you would have them do to you. Seek and you shall find; knock and the door will be open to you. Love your enemy. Do good to those who hate you." I repeated what I said that day. I wanted them to understand why I came from the Father. I longed for the love of the Father to dwell in their hearts. My Father desires hearts of flesh, not hearts of stone.

I waved to the children and invited them to gather around me.

"If you welcome these little ones, you welcome me. Whatever you do to the least of these, you do it to me." I continued to walk among them. The time was drawing near. I must leave them.

"In my Father's house, there is room for all," I said to them. "I must go and prepare a place for you."

They had embraced my teachings. My followers were already living the life my Father had called them to live.

I gazed at the faces that surrounded me. I saw some familiar faces standing at the edge of the crowd. My centurion had come. Gaius was not wearing his armor. He had his family with him, including his servant who I healed. I waved them forward.

"Master," Gaius said as he came to me. "My family… I have told them about you. They wanted so much to see you."

I blessed his wife and children. His elderly servant fell at my feet.

"Thank you," he said. I laid my hands on his head in blessing and wiped the tears from his eyes.

I turned to Gaius. "I will call on you, Gaius. You will be needed."

He bowed to me. "Say but the word, Lord."

There were other people here I needed to speak to. A woman, who was heavily veiled, held the hand of her young, beaming son.

"Claudia, you have nothing to fear from me or these people," I said to her.

The wife of Pontius Pilate slipped off her headscarf. She lifted her eyes to mine. "Lord, we of all people, are not worthy of you."

I put my hand on her shoulder, "I welcome all who come to me."

Her son Pilo was close to tears.

"I'm so sorry, for what my Tata did," he said, barely able to get the words out as he choked back his emotions.

"Do not worry Pilo, all is forgiven him."

"Go home, Claudia, for you carry with you the truth you have learned from me. Your time will come to enter into the fullness as my disciple."

"I fear for my husband and for his safety. Ill winds blow from Rome. Pontius trembles with each communication from the Emperor," she said. "Just this week he got a notice. He dared not open it in my presence. It's hard to trust anyone."

"Trust me," I said as I clasped her hands in mine.

I moved out a little further to the edge of the crowd where I noticed a centurion keeping a close eye on me as I spoke to Claudia. She followed me.

"My husband insisted that I not travel alone. This is Centurion Cornelius. He commands the soldiers from Italia who provide protection for our family."

"Cornelius, peace be with you," I greeted him.

Centurion Cornelius, an older man in his fifties, probably appreciated the guard duty rather than taking part in the risky adventure of keeping the Pax Romana. He smiled at me and took a long look at my wounds. He glanced at Gaius, who nodded to him.

"Greetings, sir, I brought my Lady here at her insistence. I can see why. I've never heard you preach before," Cornelius said. "I have a large household. You must come and speak to them."

"I will send one who has heard my voice. He will bring my word to you and your household."

The afternoon sun beamed down on the crowd. No one was hungry. They brought plenty of food, which they shared with each other. My purpose in meeting my disciples was to strengthen their faith.

I turned to those closest to me and invited them to gather with me, in a few days, on the hillside in Bethany. It would be my last gathering with them.

42. Letters

ALEXANDER SAT ON THE FAR SIDE of my desk, stylus in hand. I needed him to write a letter requesting Yosef of Arimathea to meet with me. Alexander spoke and wrote in more languages than anyone I knew. I only had to dictate the words and Alexander would compose them in the required language. This letter he would write in Hebrew.

Yosef was one of the few members of the Sanhedrin that I felt I could communicate with in a sane and non-partisan manner. He knew well the political landscape and was not afraid of Caiaphas or me.

I began, "Yosef, I request your presence in Caesarea to discuss a matter concerning recent events." Short to the point, that is all I needed to say. I signed and pressed my seal on the letter. Alexander rolled the small scroll and waited for my next missive.

This letter required diplomacy, not my strong suite. Fortunately, Alexander could make my words sound diplomatic.

"Alexander, the letter is going to Herod Antipas in Galilee. I'll trust you will compose it appropriately, perhaps in Hebrew. There is a centurion by the name of Gaius Marius with the Sepphoris division. I want Herod to transfer him to my command. Include in the letter that I was impressed with his service in Jerusalem during the Passover. That should provide Herod a reason for my request."

"Yes, sir. Anything else?"

I need to send a warm welcome to Lucius Vitellius as Legate of Syria. Add that I look forward to a meeting with him at a suitable time for both of us."

"Should I write this one in Latin, sir?"

"Yes. Compose the letters and I will seal them."

Alexander began to work his magic on my words. I still had that troublesome letter from Tiberius yet to answer.

****

Later…

I heard voices coming from the palace entrance. Claudia and Pilo had returned from their mysterious trip to Galilee.

"I'm happy to have you back," I greeted them.

Pilo ran to me and threw his arms around my waist. "Tata, Yeshua forgives you!"

"Oh, did you see him?"

"Yes, dear we did," Claudia responded

"You should have told me that's why you were going there. I might have gone with you."

"I didn't know that's why we were called to go until we saw him."

"Called? What do you mean? Who called you?" I asked. This wasn't making sense.

"It was just a voice urging me to go with our son to Galilee. I knew you wouldn't understand."

"You're right about that. I don't."

I saw Cornelius standing in the entrance. I waved him forward. "Did you meet Yeshua of Nazareth too?"

"Yes, sir, I did."

"What do you make of him? Is he alive?"

"Yes, sir, he is. He speaks well of you."

"Does he now?"

"Yes, sir."

Maybe I can get him to go and visit Tiberius.

"I'd like to speak with him myself. I'm hoping Yosef of Arimathea can arrange it. I have a letter for him."

"Yosef was at the gathering on the hill near Lake Tiberius," Claudia said as she headed to the dining area. "I think they are staying at the inn near the road. They traveled with our caravan."

"They?" I asked as I join her in the eating area.

"Nicodemus was with him."

"Perhaps they can come here before they continue their journey tomorrow. Cornelius, I know you are probably anxious to get back to your family, but could you stop by the inn and deliver my inquiry to Yosef? Tell him I'd like to see both he and Nicodemus before they leave the area."

"Certainly, sir," Cornelius replied.

Alexander was still sitting at my desk listening to the conversation. He handed Cornelius the letter for Yosef.

"We will continue in the morning, Alexander."

***

The next day

"Sir, Yosef of Arimathea, and Nicodemus from the Sanhedrin are here to see you, as you requested."

"Show them in, Alexander."

"Yes, sir."

The two Pharisees looked half their age, or so it seemed. Their faces glowed under their stark white beards. They greet me with smiles that I rarely saw on the faces of members of the Sanhedrin.

"Please, gentlemen, have a seat. I have something to discuss with you. It is not related to the work of the Sanhedrin."

"You should know, Prefect, that we have taken our leave as members of the Sanhedrin," Yosef told me.

"Oh, what has transpired to cause that…or can I guess?"

"Well, sir, I think you can probably guess, but there was another incident that triggered our departure. Caiaphas had me under house arrest for providing a dignified burial for our brother Yeshua," Yosef said.

"I had no idea."

"He would have done the same to me, but he couldn't find me," Nicodemus added.

The two men shared a laugh. It looked as though they were delighted to be out from under the rule of Caiaphas.

"I have received a request from the Emperor asking me to send the Galilean healer to him. I was hoping that perhaps you could relate this to your Yeshua, who is, by all accounts, very much alive again."

"Yeshua is alive, Prefect, but not as you and I are. He is beyond this life to a new and glorious one. One, which he told us a few days ago, he would be living with his Father very soon if not already," Nicodemus explained.

"How do I tell that to the Emperor?"

I sat back in my chair and gazed at the scroll from the Emperor. I re-read Tiberius' request. I have not revealed to the two Pharisees my encounter with the Nazarene in Emmaus. I had hoped to persuade them to speak to him, perhaps achieve a favorable response. Apparently, they weren't willing to bring the request to Yeshua or they couldn't.

"Prefect, is there something troubling you?" Yosef asked.

"My response to the letter would be more complicated if your Yeshua will not present himself to the Emperor."

"You could write to the Emperor and tell him exactly what happened," Yosef said.

"I need to remain in the Emperor's favor."

The two Pharisees looked at each other and then back at me.

"Is that your primary concern, Prefect?" Nicodemus asked.

"All things are issued to the provinces as a result of being in the Emperor's good graces. So, one's province must be in good order, one's judgments must be without question, and all taxes collected and forwarded to Rome."

"You killed an innocent man. Is that what you are afraid the Emperor will discover?"

I got up from the desk and walked to the portico. *I can't admit to them that they are right. I need to end this meeting now.*

"Yosef, Nicodemus, thank you for coming. I'm sorry if I unduly delayed your journey. Safe passage."

"Good day, Prefect," they said in unison.

It was urgent that I rid myself of this Yeshua of Nazareth affair. I considered that it might be safer to tell Tiberius that the Nazarene was dead, without providing an explanation. I watched out the south portico as the two men proceeded on foot for Jerusalem. I would go there myself in about a week for the Jewish Feast of Shavuot and more insufferable crowds.

43. The Encounter

CLAUDIA TOLD ME SHE WAS CONSIDERING becoming a Jew so that she could be a full disciple of Yeshua. She said that she would be discrete and not raise the suspicions of Romans or Jews. It was an admirable attempt to appease my concerns I expressed after Yeshua's death in Jerusalem.

She sat up in bed reading by the light of her lamp. She read from a scroll that Joanna gave her. It was late, and I was trying to sleep. Her whispered voice kept me awake.

"Pontius, are you asleep?"

"How can I possibly be asleep?"

"I'm sorry, but you must listen to what the prophet Isaiah wrote many years ago. It's about the Jewish Messiah. Who does this sound like…?"

I rolled onto my back and listened to my wife, the daughter of the Divine Tiberius Caesar, read from a Jewish scroll. The prophecy details the suffering of a man, the Jews assume, is their messiah. I knew what Claudia was thinking.

"So, I was doomed from the start to play a role in the fulfillment of the Jews' messianic prophecies. I'm the one who caused the man's suffering and death."

Claudia looked down at me. "It doesn't say anything about that. It just says...*ours were the sufferings he bore. He was pierced through for our offenses...*"

"Enough, Claudia, give me that. Put your lamp out and go to sleep." I grasped the scroll from her and threw it on the floor.

"Pontius!"

"Now! I'm tired."

"Ohhh!"

The light went out, and the room plunged into darkness. I laid there for a few moments. I was wide awake. I could tell by her breathing that Claudia was already asleep.

I got up and wandered to the southwest portico, which looked out over the pool and the sea just beyond it. The image of the half-moon shimmered in the pool's still water. The waves of the seas caught the moon's light as they rhythmically washed ashore.

The sound of drunken voices broke the hypnotic spell of the waves. The shouts emanated from the ships moored at the port further down the shore. The torches on the wharf lit the ships tied to the dock.

A warm breeze blew a fresh aroma around me. I heard a whisper nearby. I couldn't tell what was being said or who was speaking. I sensed I was not alone. I reached for my sword. I didn't have it. I spotted the scabbard on my desk. I heard the voice again. It was clearer this time, "Ponti."

"Who's there? Who dares call me Ponti."

My heart was in my throat. My guards kept watch outside the palace. I was alone. *I must defend myself.* I made a dash to my desk and grabbed my sword from the scabbard and a torch from the wall. It was quiet again. I heard only the sound of my own breathing.

"Ponti, fear not."

"Guards! Guards!" *I hope they can hear me.*

"Who are you? Show yourself."

"I am, who I am."

"You speak foolishness. Who are you?"

The water in the pool sloshed. I edged toward the southwest portico. All the torches around the pool were suddenly ablaze.

"Guards! Guards come at once!"

"Peace be with you, Ponti."

There was a figure in a white light standing at the far end of the pool. He waved to me, inviting me to join him. I hesitated.

"Come. Fear not." His voice was familiar. *Is it the Nazarene?*

I inched down the stairs and gripped my sword. I was about to encounter a dead man who lives. He might be here to revenge his death. As I got closer, I could clearly see that it was Yeshua of Nazareth. A white light emanated from him. Very strange. He smiled and extended his hand to me. I could see the nail wound.

"Peace be with you."

The sword dropped from my hand. I took his. He was solid. He was not a ghost.

"What do you want from me, Yeshua?"

"It is you who wanted to see me."

"How could you know that? Did Yosef or Nicodemus tell you?"

"I know."

I felt myself relax, a little. He seemed pleasant enough. I no longer felt at risk.

"No one has called me *Ponti* since I was a kid. That's my old family name."

"I know."

"Thank you for straightening my son's foot. It means a great deal to us. If I had only known before…I wouldn't have…"

"You are welcome. I came to bring everyone to wholeness. I didn't want you to know at the time.

"I don't understand; I was ready to let you go… "

Yeshua smiled at me. "Be at peace, Pontius. Do not trouble yourself."

I might as well get to the point now that he is here.

"Yeshua, I got a letter from the Emperor. He has heard of you. He wants me to send the Galilean healer to him. I can pay for your passage to Italia on a ship that leaves in the morning."

"No, I am to return to my Father."

"Can you go after you've seen the Emperor?"

"No. You will send a message to him."

"Me? What exactly do I tell him?"

"Tell the Emperor what took place."

"What? That I deemed you innocent of any crime against Rome, but that I caved into the threats from Caiaphas and had you crucified, and then you rose from the dead."

"Yes."

"I can't tell him the truth; he'll have my head."

"Do you not demand the truth from those under your command?"

"Well, yes."

"Then, you too must be truthful to those who command you."

"That truth could get me killed."

"Or set you free."

Yeshua walked to the edge of the pool, took off his sandals and sat down. He kicked his nail-holed feet in the water and patted the space beside him, inviting me to sit. I put the torch I held in a holder at the side of the pool and sat beside him.

"This feels odd. I was assured that Friday that you were dead, and on Monday I was told you were alive," I said to him. "And here you are."

Yeshua looked at the water as if he was trying to formulate the right words. "It was as it should be. I forgive you."

"No eye for an eye?"

"That's not what I taught my disciples."

I saw something out of the corner of my eye to my right, it was someone in a long white robe, an illuminance figure, I couldn't tell if it was male or female. I thought of Claudia's word *Being.*

"Who is that?" I asked Yeshua.

"My angel."

"What is your angel doing?"

"Getting the scrolls ready so we can write our story."

"We...write?"

The angel stepped aside and revealed a white table with two chairs behind it. There appeared to be a stack of parchment on the table. The angel spoke to Yeshua in a language I'd never heard before, but strangely enough, I could understand.

"All is ready, Lord."

The angel was immediately at our side, guiding us both to the table. Yeshua sat on my right and handed me a stylus.

"What are we going to write?"

"Our story, in its fullness and in truth. You tell it from your point of view, and I will tell mine."

I hesitated. "I don't know if I remember everything."

"It will all come to you as we write."

I put the stylus to the parchment. The words began to flow. It all flooded back. I looked over at Yeshua, his face was focused, and beads of sweat were forming on his brow.

The angel offered him a drink, which he took. He glanced at me and nodded. "I'm fine. The memories are intense."

I went back to my own writing. I wanted to change the facts, let him go, but that's not what happen. I turned to him.

"I'm sorry. It was my fault. I should have followed my instincts. I knew you did nothing to deserve the punishment you endured."

Yeshua turned to me and put his hand on my shoulder. He said nothing. A wave of peace came over me.

I wrote and wrote until there was nothing more to say. I put the stylus down. The angel brought me a drink and rolled my last scroll.

"I am finished," I said as I turned to Yeshua.

"So am I," he replied. "There is one last thing."

Yeshua signaled to the angel. The angel approached me and ran his or her fingers through the front of my hair. I started laughing, "What are you doing?"

"Just cutting a piece or two," Yeshua said

The angel clipped a couple of my hard-to-grow-locks, tied them together with a piece of string and put them inside the scroll.

"Some day all will know you are my disciple."

"But I'm not…"

The area was suddenly dark. The torches extinguished, except the one I brought with me. Yeshua and his angel were gone. I was alone. The scrolls were neatly rolled and stacked on the table. My head was foggy. I had no idea of how long I had been there writing with Yeshua. I was exhausted and needed to go to bed.

***

I opened my eyes and sat up in bed. I looked over at Claudia; she was sleeping soundly. I had the strangest dream, at least I thought was a dream. I got up and looked out the window. The moon was sinking into the sea. Everything was as it should be, except me. Nothing was routine after the week of Passover. The death of Yeshua of Nazareth had turned my life upside down. Now, I was having nightmares about him. As I went back to bed, all I could think of was how to appease the Emperor's request and not lie in the process.

***

Morning

"Claudia, where's my sword? I have my scabbard but it is empty."

"Wherever you left it. Have you checked the office?"

"Yes. I've just spent half my morning preparation time looking for it. I don't feel dressed without it. I can't imagine leaving it somewhere."

"Why do you have to dress in your armor? You're home," Claudia said.

"You never know when I might have to defend us against intruders."

"The palace is surrounded by soldiers," she pointed out.

Alexander entered the office to begin the day's work. I was still wandering about looking high and low for my sword. The disturbing night had left me feeling dragged-out.

"Good morning, sir,"

"Yes, Alexander. Have you seen my sword? I seem to have misplaced it, and I have no idea where."

Alexander looked around the office and then walked to the west portico. "Sir, I believe it is down there on the far side of the pool."

I joined him on the top step. I remembered last night's dream. *Maybe it wasn't a dream.* I felt dizzy as though I was about to fall. I reached out and grabbed Alexander's arm.

"Sir, are you all right? You look pale. Sit here, I'll get you some water."

If it wasn't a dream, what was it? I wish I could think. Think, think…what happened last night?

Alexander brought me a refreshing drink. The world was no longer spinning

He went poolside to retrieve my sword. He stopped beside the white table and gathered up an armful of scrolls. He brought them to me at the top of the stairs.

"What are these, sir? Some are in your hand, and well, I don't recognize the other hand, and it is in Aramaic. Who wrote those?"

"Just take them down to the record room and put them in a safe place." The events of the previous night were beginning to come back to me. I decided to keep it to myself.

44. Ascension

Some days later

Jerusalem to Bethany

THE UPPER ROOM WAS OVERCROWDED, but that pleased me. My family including my mother, older brother James and his family, my apostles, my Bethany friends, the women who have been with me since the beginning, Yosef, and Nicodemus were there. It was time for me to take them for a walk to a hill near the town of Bethany. I had mixed feelings about what was about to happen. I was going home to my Father. It meant that I must leave them for the second time.

I donned the generous hood on the robe that Pontius and his son gave me. It allowed me to pass through the streets of Jerusalem unrecognized. My disciples were the only people who needed to see me.

As we walked up the hill, through the Mount of Olives, I turned to face Jerusalem one last time. The Temple dominated the view. I had a lump in my throat.

"Jerusalem, Jerusalem, how I have longed to gather you under my wing, as a hen gathers her chicks, but alas you would not! There will come a time when not one stone will be lying on top of another. If only you had been aware of the hour of your visitation." I wiped the tears from my face. I couldn't bear it.

I turned and continued the walk to Bethany. Lazarus walked beside me with his arm around my shoulder. He knew how much the Temple meant to me. He was with me the first time I saw it; it was during Passover when we were young and so full of dreams.

My disciples followed me. My Mother and John were on my right, Lazarus and his sisters were on my left. Simon Peter and James were slightly behind me. They chattered among themselves. They discussed different topics but mostly around what was going to happen next. Mother tightened her grip on my arm. She knew. I put my hand on hers and pulled her closer to me. Mother's eyes filled with tears. I hugged her.

As we approached the bottom of the hill, I gathered my friends around me one last time. I cleared my throat of the emotion that was rising within me. I loved them. I loved them all. Leaving them was harder than I imagined. I placed mother's hand on John's arm. It was time.

"There are many rooms in my Father's house. I am going to prepare a place for each of you. I have come from the Father and am going back to the Father. Remain in my love. For I am in you and you are in me. Be as one, as the Father and I are one. Do not look for me for I am going where you cannot go. But, someday you will follow me."

"Remain in Jerusalem until the Holy Spirit comes. Then, go forth into the whole world, indeed to the ends of the earth, baptizing them in the Name of the Father, and of the Son and the Holy Spirit. I will be with you, even until the end of time."

I continued up the hill. A cloud descended around me. My friends could no longer see me. I am in the home of my Father.

45. The Dreaded Task

Caesarea Maritima

Evening the same day

THE SINGLE LAMP ON MY DESK FLICKERED in the breeze from the sea. I fumbled the stylus between my fingers. I didn't want to write the letter. I didn't know what to include. I could just tell a little of the truth, but which part of it should I tell Tiberius? My error in judgment? The Nazarene's resurrection?

I pushed away from the desk and strolled to the portico. I looked out on the sea and the pool. My eyes trained on the spot where I encountered him. I never told Claudia about it. I didn't want her to pressure me to become a follower of the Nazarene. That would compromise my position. No, things needed to stay the way they were. I confess, though, he was hard to ignore.

I leaned against a column and agonized over what to write on the scroll. I had to give Tiberius an answer. A familiar breeze swirled around me. The hairs on the back of my neck bristled. A shiver went through me. I looked across the room at the-the scroll on my desk. It became clear what to say in the letter.

I sat down at my desk, picked up the stylus and wrote a complete account of the trial, and later resurrection of Yeshua of Nazareth. I wrote the truth. When I finished, I rolled the scroll up, poured the wax on it and pressed it with the seal of my ring.

I prepared it for transportation to the Emperor on Capri, to be sent first thing the next morning. Alexander will probably wonder why I would write to the Emperor without his assistance. He frequently corrected my style to be more appropriate for the Emperor. Even though I wrote with confidence, I was not sure of the wisdom of telling Tiberius, the truth about the Galilean healer. I was taking a chance that the Emperor would believe the resurrection story. I also told him that the Galilean straightened Pilo's foot. That should add some credibility to the story. I gave him one recommendation that the Senate consider declaring Yeshua of Nazareth, a god. I wasn't sure how far that will go. If the Senate agreed, it would make belief in him much less dangerous for Romans; my wife and son included.

Part Two
The Way

46. A New Commander

Several days later

CENTURION CORNELIUS ARRIVED IN MY OFFICE; he had another centurion with him, Centurion Gaius Marius from Galilee. Herod Antipas had granted consideration for my request.

"Greetings, Centurions. I am pleased to see you, Centurion Marius, please have a seat. Cornelius, thank you for showing him in."

"Good day, sir. I don't know exactly why you sent for me, but I received an order from my commander to report for duty here in Caesarea," Centurion Marius said.

"Yes, I did send for you. Let me get right to the point for discussion. I need a new Tribune of the forces here in Judea. I was impressed with your conduct during the Passover feast, and I want you in charge."

"Sir, I'm not sure what to say. The last time we spoke you were not pleased with my conduct, as I recall."

"Yes, yes that is correct. However, since then new information has come to my attention that sufficiently clarified the incident at the tomb of Yeshua of Nazareth."

"I see, sir." Marius crunched his eyebrows.

Centurion Marius was quiet for a moment. He took a few glances at me and pressed his lips together. "Prefect, I'm not sure I am the man for the job."

"And why is that centurion?"

"To be honest with you, sir, I have accepted the teachings of the Nazarene who was crucified that day before Passover. I will not kill innocent people, even if ordered to do so."

The centurion was looking me in the eye. I knew he was telling me the truth and was taking a significant risk in doing so.

"I'll make every effort not issue such an order to you. I appreciate your candor."

Marius still did not look convinced. He didn't want the job. I could have ordered him to do it, but I did not want to have to do that.

Marius glanced at Cornelius, who remained expressionless. He was not going to help him with this decision. Gaius closed his eyes. I wasn't sure what he was doing. His lips moved slightly, he was praying. I managed to withhold my laughter. I looked at Cornelius, his eyes were downcast.

Gaius Marius finally spoke, "My family is in Sepphoris, sir. I'd have to move them here."

He's stalling. I know he is. I should give him the benefit of the doubt.

"Fine, I'll give you a week to make arrangements to relocate them. I'm sure Cornelius will assist you in acquiring accommodations. Can I expect you to take up your command in Jerusalem during the coming Feast of Shavuot?"

"Yes, sir."

I'd have to watch my new commander. He may be an honest man, but would he carry out the orders I give him? That question remained.

47. Shavuot

Jerusalem

Jewish Feast of Shavuot

JERUSALEM WAS IN A BETTER MOOD during Shavuot or Pentecost. The Jews celebrated their first harvest and their law. They presented offerings to their God in the Temple. I leaned against a pillar and watched the Jews going through their rituals in the outer courtyard of the Temple and then get a blessing from the High Priest. Caiaphas was in his realm. The incense from every prayer offering filled the air and drifted up to the palace. It irritated my throat.

I liked this feast, the greater the fruits of their labor, the more taxes I got in the coffers; not a bad deal, at least for me.

My tax collectors lined up in the Praetorium to turn in the taxes they had collected so far. I returned to my desk and proceeded to add it up and mark off the names of those who had paid, hopefully, in full. There was still an enormous debt on the aqueduct. The Temple funds only paid a portion of it, although, by the acrimonious reception that got, one would think it paid the entire cost. It didn't. I had to raise local taxes to pay the rest. The Jews complain endlessly about it. You'd think they would show me some gratitude for bringing much-needed freshwater to their Holy City.

As I collect the money from my tax collectors, I noticed Nicodemus standing behind and off to the left-hand side of the line-up. I motioned him forward.

"Good day, Nicodemus."

"Good day, Prefect. May I speak to you in private?"

"I'm rather busy as you can see. We can talk later."

"What I have to say won't take long, and it is time sensitive."

I agreed to meet with the Pharisee in my quarters.

***

"Prefect, I am here to extend an invitation to you and your wife and son to join us in the Upper Room for our Pentecost. I believe you know where it is. Simon Peter, the leader of the Lord Yeshua's followers, asked me to extend this invitation to you."

I'm stunned by his words. I, a Roman Prefect, invited to celebrate a Jewish feast? Not likely.

"Nicodemus, while I appreciate the nature of this invitation, it would not be appropriate for me to attend a Jewish feast. Who is this Simon Peter? I've never heard of the man."

"I understand, Prefect. Simon Peter is the leader of the Lord's followers and does the Lord's bidding."

I felt someone touch my shoulder. I turned to see Claudia behind me. Her eyes beseeched me; she wanted to go with Nicodemus.

I shook my head, "No, Claudia. I will not have you attending a Jewish feast."

"But, husband, I would be discrete; no one will know it is me or where I am going."

"I said no, Claudia." I was aware of the presence of Nicodemus and that he was witnessing my discussion with my wife.

"Nicodemus, you have my answer."

"Prefect, Lady Claudia, Shalom," Nicodemus, his face reddened, bowed his head and departed.

I turned my attention back to my wife, "Claudia, don't ever argue with me in front of other people. That was not appropriate."

"Pontius, why are you refusing me?"

"I have been very patient with you and your obsession with Yeshua of Nazareth. I know he healed our son, but until I get a positive response from the appeal I've made to Tiberius the answer is no. I consider it far too dangerous to allow you to become a Jew or be that man's disciple."

"Appeal? What appeal?"

I realized that I just told her something she didn't know. "I've responded to a request from the Emperor concerning the Nazarene. He has somehow learned of the healer from Galilee. I…"

She backed away from me, holding her hand to her face. Her cheeks were glowing red. She ran to the bedroom.

"Claudia!" I followed her. "Claudia, did you have something to do with that information getting back to Tiberius?"

With her back to me, she nodded in silence and choked back her tears. "It was months ago after I came back from my first trip to Galilee. I wrote to him about Yeshua's healing powers that I witnessed while I was at the edge of the crowd. I never thought…"

"You never thought about the consequences of your actions. How could you do such a thing behind my back?"

"Pontius…it…it was an innocence letter to my... I never expected that you would eventually send such a man as Yeshua to the cross."

"Do you have any idea what a difficult situation you've put me in?"

"No! Please Pontius, how could I have known? I did try and stop you from crucifying him, but you wouldn't listen."

"That's enough, Claudia!"

"What appeal did you make to the Emperor? What was it about? There's something you're not telling me, Pontius."

I turned and went to the living area. Pilo was standing outside his room. He had a pout on his lips. Claudia followed stomping her feet behind me.

I headed back out to the Praetorium. I had taxes to count.

***

The line-up of tax collectors had grown. That was a good sign. The more money I collected to send back to Rome the greater my fortunes would be with the Emperor. I pushed the whole discussion with Claudia out of my mind.

I had a sense that someone was watching me. I glanced around and spotted the Galilean centurion standing a few feet away. I motioned him forward.

"Are you reporting for duty Centurion or should I say, Commander?"

"I am, sir."

"Good to have you here, Commander Marius. You know what I expect. Preserve the Pax Romana at all times, report any suspicious activities to me, and put down any potential uprisings. You have your orders, Commander."

"Yes, sir,"

My new Tribune, Chief of the Army snapped his heels and left the Praetorium. That was one problem solved. *I must ask him if he knows Simon Peter. I want to know if I should be concerned about him.*

As I continued my work, I heard the door of the residence open and close. I looked over my shoulder. No one was there.

By mid-morning, I had taken in so much tax money that I needed Alexander to help me carry it into the palace and secure it. He helped write up the official record and when he thought I wasn't looking, checked my summation of the returns.

***

The mid-day meal was prepared and set out on the table. I reclined on the lounge and waited for Claudia and Pilo to join me. Pilo came out of his room and reclined across from me.

"Where's your Mater?"

He shrugged, "I don't know, Tata. I was in my room doing my numbers and letters for school."

"I want to see them when you're done, Pilo."

"Yes, Tata. I'll bring them to you."

I kept looking at the curtains to the bedroom. I assumed that my wife was not speaking to me again. I put some food on her plate.

"Pilo, take this plate of fruit and fish to your Mater. She might be hungry."

"Yes, Tata."

Pilo got up, took the plate and went to the bedroom. He pushed the curtain aside and then turned to me. "She's not here, Tata."

I gritted my teeth and glared at the bedroom. *She didn't go...*

A sudden gust of wind interrupted my thoughts. It blew hard against the palace door and pushed it open. Cushions on Claudia's empty lounge tumbled to the floor. My manservant hurried to secure the door.

"Is there a storm coming?" I asked.

"No, sir. It is perfectly clear out."

"Odd," I noted. The wind died down as quickly as it came. Pilo got up from his lounge and went to the window, then he unbolted the door and ran outside. I pursued him.

"Pilo, come back here."

By the time I went out I couldn't see him. "Guard, get my steed and Commander Marius." *My wife has disappeared and now, so has my son.*

I met the Commander in the courtyard. He had my steed. "Commander, we need to go to the house that the Nazarene's followers occupy. I believe my wife is there, and my son is headed there."

"Do you know where it is?" Commander Marius asked me.

"Yes, I passed it once."

***

We rode with haste but with care. We looked for Pilo among the crowds. I reined my horse to a stop and checked around the square near the market. *How can I possibly find my boy is this crowd?* The house where I encountered the Galilean's mother was a short distance away.

"Down that street, Commander. It's the middle building on the right."

I paid no attention to the crowd shouting insults at me. I had to find my wife and son. They put themselves in danger. I felt the sweat pouring down my face, and my mouth was getting dry. I could hardly breathe.

I pulled my steed to a stop and jumped off. I glanced at the house. The upstairs shutters were open. Some hung from one end as though they were sheared off. The door was wide open. I started to enter when Commander Marius put out his arm to stop me.

"It's best if I go. Here, keep my scabbard for me. I don't need to be armed."

"Are you sure? They might attack you."

"No, sir, they won't."

I waited impatiently between the two steeds. There was no sound coming from the house. I heard crowd noises coming from the direction of the Temple, a short distance away.

"Commander, are they here?"

Marius came out of the house tight-lipped. He shook his head.

"No, sir. There is no one in the house. They've all gone."

"Where…where could they have gone?"

"Perhaps we should check the Temple. I can go into the Court of the Gentiles as long as I'm not armed."

We mounted our horses and raced to the Temple. I dismounted. Crowds streamed by us. I had no protection. I left in such a hurry that I didn't bring Cornelius and his soldiers.

"It would be best if you remain outside of the Temple grounds, sir. I'll go," Gaius shouted above the din.

I leaned my head against my steed hoping no one recognized me. Some people already had. They issued terse warnings not to enter the Temple, or they'd kill me. I had no doubt they would. I placed my hand on my scabbard just in case. I found myself praying to the gods that the commander would find my family quickly.

Out of the corner of my eye, I saw a glint; before I could react, Cornelius was between the attacker and me. He quickly subdued and disarmed the man. Why he didn't kill him, I didn't know.

"Cornelius, am I relieved you're here."

He sheathed his weapon. "You left without me, sir. I'm just doing my job, sir, protecting you and your family."

He stepped aside. Claudia and Pilo were behind him.

Commander Marius smiled at me. "I found them in the Temple, sir. They were listening to Simon Peter preach."

I glared at Claudia. I did not wish to have it out with her in public.

"Well, Centurion would you please escort my family back to the palace. Commander, you're with me."

"Yes, sir."

After the commotion, the street soldiers noticed my presence and surrounded us. They took the attacker into custody. *I'll make sure he is crucified as soon as possible.*

***

"You're coming with me to the north turret."

"Why, what are you going to do to me?"

"I need to talk to you privately, and it's the only place where I can do that. Now, Claudia, come."

I grabbed her by the arm and dragged her to the north turret. We didn't use it for anything, it's more of a watch tower. It was away from our living quarters and servants. We climbed several sets of stairs.

"Let go of me. You're hurting my arm," Claudia squealed.

"Fine, but don't leave."

"I'm here aren't I?"

We got to the door, and I pushed on it. It didn't open. I gave it a kick and it flung open with a thud. I pulled Claudia around in front of me.

"Claudia, I brought you here to Judea with me to be my wife and supporter. That's what Roman wives do. For the last few weeks, you have chased after the Nazarene and his followers. It must stop now!"

"You don't understand, Pontus, I can't. I believe in him. That he is God."

"I expect you to obey me, your husband, and to worship the gods of Rome. Not the Jews' God."

My patience was wearing thin. I paced the room. Claudia, arms crossed, was standing in the middle of it. Her face was set with determination. Disobedience was grounds for divorce. However, that would not be politically expedient for me. I needed to keep Claudia as my wife to stay in the Emperor's favor.

"I have decided to send you and Pilo back to Rome. You can live in the Ponti Villa. The servants who live there have served my family for many years and will take care of you and Pilo."

"Pontius, no!"

"Silence, Claudia, if that is possible."

"Pilo will be educated there. Become a proper Roman, away from this Jewish nonsense. And you, hopefully, will regain your senses."

Claudia sniffled. The tears poured down her face. She knew she must do what I tell her. "May I go to my room now, husband?"

"Yes, and I expect to see you at dinner in proper Roman clothing. Get out of those Jewish clothes. And you will join me in the worship room before bed."

Her eyes flashed at me. She pursed her lips and turned her back to me, "I will never again worship the gods of Rome. Crucify me if you must." Claudia stepped out of the turret and slammed the door behind her. She was still my wife, legally, but the marriage was over.

**

The silence was deafening. Claudia joined me for meals but only talked to me through Pilo. He didn't understand what was going on between his parents. When I explained to him that he and his mother were going live in Rome, he cried.

I admit I still cared for Claudia. It's hard not to, she is a beautiful woman, but I could no longer tolerate her utter disrespect for my authority over her and our Roman ways. I certainly could not allow Pilo to be enculturated into any form of the Jewish religion.

The whole situation was unsettling. I hoped it would improve when we got back to Caesarea. We would leave in the morning. At least, there are a few more bedrooms in the palace living quarters. I did not look forward to sleeping on the lounge. *Claudia should sleep on it.*

My only place of refuge from the tension in the palace was out in the Praetorium. I strolled to the balcony and noticed Commander Marius and Centurion Cornelius approaching in the courtyard below. I motioned to them to join me. It might be good to have an informal chat with a couple of men. Cornelius was as close to a friend that I had in Judea, and it might be a good opportunity to get to know Gaius Marius.

"Come, have a drink with me."

"Yes, sir," they said in unison.

"That was an invitation not an order," I hollered back.

"Servant, bring some strong wine, not the watered-down stuff you serve women." Now, that was an order.

I pulled the chairs in front of my desk and invited my guests to remove their armor. "Please, let us have an informal evening chat."

My servant served three goblets of wine and provided a generous basket of grapes, figs, cheese, and pears. My men waited for me to take the first drink. I saluted them.

"Welcome to your new command, Gaius. I hope your first few days on the job haven't been too hard on you."

"No, sir. Nothing unexpected, except maybe for Lady Claudia's adventure. Which turned out satisfactorily, thanks to Cornelius."

"Yes, well, that won't happen again, I can assure you. I'm sending Claudia and Pilo to Rome. I have our family villa there, which will do nicely for them. It will be good for Pilo to receive a proper Roman education. I can't really give him that here."

Cornelius stopped in the middle of drinking his wine and lowered his hand and goblet to his lap. "Do you want me to go with them, sir? It can be a perilous journey and perhaps a risky time to be in Rome."

"Why would it be risky for them in Rome?"

"Well, sir, as you know, Rome is in a state of political uncertainty with an aging emperor but no clear successor," Cornelius said. "And I would be concerned, if I were you, about the safety of Pilo."

Cornelius was somewhat of a sage for me. I failed to listen to his words of wisdom when I first came to Judea. He advised me against putting the banners with the image of the emperor on them in Jerusalem. I disregarded his advice, and I almost had a Jewish revolt on my hands. So now, I tend to listen well to Cornelius' suggestions.

"Tell me what you are thinking, Cornelius. Why would Pilo be endangered?"

"Your wife, sir, is the granddaughter of Augustus, is she not?"

"Yes. I don't follow you."

"From what I understand, Tiberius adopted her as his daughter when her mother died. He has no living son to assume the role of Emperor upon his death."

"That's right." I leaned in a little closer to him. "Continue, Cornelius."

"There are some who are competing to be Tiberius' successor. Among them is Claudius Caligula, Tiberius' nephew. He is positioning himself to succeed Tiberius. If he is successful, there is no doubt that he will rid the empire of any perceived competitors to his line of succession. That would include your son – the great-grandson of Augustus."

The wine caught in my throat. I started to choke.

"Sir, are you all right?" Gaius patted me on my back. I struggled to get my voice back.

"Yes...I'm...fine." I paused for a minute to breathe. "Cornelius, where did you get this information? I had no idea what was going on in Rome as far as the Emperor was concerned."

"My brother, who is a Praetorian guard in the Emperor's court, has written to me about the growing political tensions in the court. As you know, guards are often aware of the politics of their stations, we just can't speak of them. My brother considers it safe to write to me about the situation on Capri."

"The thought of Pilo being in line never occurred to me. He's just a boy."

"A boy, yes. Nevertheless, he is a boy in direct line to the Emperor as is Caligula, who also is a great-grandson of Augustus.

I drained my goblet of wine. I have never feared for Pilo's life, only my own. Cornelius has made me realize another reality for my family. A much more dangerous reality than I had ever considered. I could not send Claudia and Pilo back to Rome.

"Thank you, Cornelius. I have never given a thought to my son's future because of his lineage on his mother's side. I've only been concerned about my own possible fate. It was my hope that no matter what happened to me that Claudia's relationship with Tiberius would spare her and my son. It's clear from what you have said that I need to think beyond the reign of Tiberius."

My servant refilled my wine goblet. I drained it again. I needed to get in touch with my friend Seneca, in Rome. He would understand the political landscape better than anyone I know.

***

The Next Morning

As much as I regretted having to change my decision to send Claudia and Pilo back to Rome, I dreaded even more that I had to tell her. I could just imagine the look of victory on her face. I could not, of course, reveal to her why I

---

changed my mind because any possible threat to Pilo would unnerve her.

Claudia and Pilo joined me for breakfast before we departed for Caesarea. She barely looked at me. Pilo shifted on his couch. It was time to break the tension.

"Pilo, how would you like to stay in Judea with me?"

"Oh, yes, Tata, I would, I would," he said. He got up and threw his arms around me. Claudia's mouth opened, but she didn't say a word.

"Do you think we should let mommi stay too?" *If she can speak to me through Pilo, I can play the same game.*

"Yes, Tata. Please let mommi stay too."

"Fine, Pilo. You tell mommi she can stay."

Pilo was getting wise to his parent's ways. He scrunched his face and said, "She's right here Tata, you tell her!"

I couldn't keep a straight face. Neither could Claudia. She got off her lounge, scrambled over, and settled behind me.

"I'd like some grapes please," she whispered in my ear.

I plucked a grape from the bunch in the bowl and rolled onto my back. She was resting on her elbow looking down at me. I put the grape between my teeth. Claudia leaned down to retrieve the grape. I swallowed it. Our lips touched.

"Eww." Pilo wasn't impressed with his parents kissing.

"Pilo, tell your Mater that I love her."

Pilo jumped on the two of us. "You tell her, Tata! You tell her!"

Between our laughter, Claudia whispered to me, "I'm glad I won't have to write to you from Rome to tell you about our second child."

"Huh? Are you…?"

"Yes."

I think I was in shock. In an effort to get up, I rolled off the lounge and landed in a heap on the floor. "Well, that wonderful news now isn't it."

"What Tata? What's wonderful?"

I was finally on my feet. Pilo sat next to Claudia. I patted his head. "You're going to have a brother or sister."

"I don't want a sister, just a brother, please."

"We'll accept whichever one God gives us, Pilo," Claudia said.

I pursed my lips.

"Please, Pontius, let me have my faith. You don't have to join us."

I had already lost the battle.

"Yes, I suppose. You can believe whatever you want to believe."

Claudia stood in front of me and said, "Thank you." She put her head on my chest. I wrapped my arms around her. Pilo wrapped himself around our legs. I had my family back. The marriage was on.

"Excuse me, sir. I hope I'm not interrupting something."

"Yes, Cornelius, you are. What is it?" I turned to see his silhouette in the doorway.

"The carriage and your steed are prepared. The guards wait to escort you and your family to Caesarea, sir."

I stepped away from Claudia. My face felt hot. She giggled. Cornelius stifled a smile.

"We're coming."

"Excellent, sir."

I brushed against Cornelius on my way out. He knew what was going on. I had my suspicions that he set me up for this reconciliation. Pilo in line for Emperor – I'm sure he made that one up. Good one, though. I fell for it.

48. Cornelius' Dinner Party

Three Years Later

Caesarea Maritima

I WATCHED FROM THE BALCONY as Pilo mastered the moves with his steed. He was practicing for the equestrian event in the Greek Olympiad. At nine, he was little young to qualify for the games, but he was keen to practice. In a year, he would be able to compete with local boys.

I heard a giggle and the patter of young feet headed in my direction as my daughter, little Claudia, ran from her mother's arms. She was the image of my wife. Dark eyes, black hair, and when she wasn't laughing, a pouty mouth.

"Tata, Tata," she squealed as she reached up to me. I snatched her up in my arms and pointed to Pilo out on the riding field next to the palace.

"Look, Pilo is riding and doing tricks with his horse," I said.

She squirmed in my arms eager to go to her brother. "Pilo, Pilo," she said clapping her hands.

Claudia took her from me saying, "Cornelius is here, and he wants to invite us to his home for dinner this evening."

I turned to see Cornelius in his toga, he was off duty,

"Good afternoon, Cornelius. Dinner? Love to."

"That's good, sir. I am expecting another guest as well. I hope you will enjoy meeting him."

"Who might that be?"

"Simon Peter, the leader of the followers of Yeshua of Nazareth. I invited him to come and speak at my house. He agreed. He is arriving from Joffa in a few hours."

"I've heard that name before. Hasn't Herod been after him?"

"Yes, even caught him a couple of times, but Peter escaped from his jail."

"Escaped? So that's why Caiaphas sent word to me that if this Peter entered my territory that I was to arrest him. I told him that I would not unless of course, he broke Roman law. He hasn't has he?"

Cornelius laughed, "No sir, he hasn't."

"Good, then I look forward to meeting him."

"Cornelius, are you interested in the Nazarene?"

"Yes, sir. I had been ever since I met him when I accompanied Claudia to Galilee soon after his resurrection. I have been praying to the Jewish God and giving alms to the poor people in the city."

I looked at Claudia and back at Cornelius. "So, I'm surrounded by Yeshua believers am I?"

The two of them laughed.

"You do know that the Senate turned down my petition to declare Yeshua, a god so Romans could worship him, don't you?

"Yes, sir."

"Then you understand the danger you could both be in, should you be caught? I mean, I'm not saying I would turn either one of you in, but someone could find out."

"Peter is being escorted by Gaius Marius and some of my servants, sir. He'll be incognito. No one will know."

"Don't tell me Commander Marius is a believer too?"

Claudia and Cornelius both laughed.

"I am surrounded."

"You may as well surrender, Pontius," Claudia said.

"Not a chance."

***

Claudia and I went to the house of Cornelius and his family on foot as his villa was near the palace. His home was located up a small hill. We had been there for informal occasions and dinners.

I expected that it was going to be an interesting gathering, to say the least. I had heard the name Simon Peter from different sources. I was eager to check him out, mainly out of concern but also out of curiosity. If Herod imprisoned him twice and he escaped, he might indeed be a threat to our security. With two of my most trusted soldiers there, I figured Claudia and I would not be endangered. I wore my scabbard under my toga just in case.

Cornelius and his wife met us at we entered their home. The reception area was crowded with Romans,

Greeks, and Jews. It looked as though Cornelius had invited half the population of Caesarea.

"This way, Prefect," Cornelius said.

There was a man in the center of a crowd of people who were listening to him. Tall and big for a Jew, I thought, as the man turned to me with his hand extended.

"Prefect, this is Simon Peter bar Jona, Apostle of Yeshua of Nazareth," said Cornelius.

"Simon Peter pleased to meet you," I said as I shook his hand."

"Most people just call me Peter now, Prefect. I'm glad to finally meet you," Peter responded.

The crowd was looking on; I could see some whispering to each other. I felt uneasy. I was expecting a small dinner party with Cornelius and his wife. With the large gathering, word of me meeting with Peter could get out to the wrong people. I wanted to leave, but in courtesy to my hosts, I also felt compelled to stay.

"Please everyone, let us moved to the dining hall. Peter will speak to us after the meal," Cornelius announced.

The seating arrangements were such that Peter sat on my right between Cornelius and me. Cornelius began the meal, not with a salute to the Emperor, but with an invocation to the Jewish God. The prayer ended with everyone saying "Amen."

"If it is any comfort, Prefect, some of the Lord's disciples were against me coming to a Roman home," Peter whispered to me. My discomfort was showing.

"Why did you come?" I asked him.

"The Lord gave me a dream that I should go to the home of the Centurion Cornelius."

"You have telling dreams like my wife?"

Peter smiled at me. "And what did your wife dream?" he said, looking past me at Claudia.

"Not to crucify your Yeshua, which leads me to ask you why you are so pleased to meet me?"

"Because without his death, there would have been no resurrection. Besides, you have encountered him since his resurrection, haven't you?

"How did you know that?"

"The Lord told me. He has forgiven you and me."

"What did you do?"

"It was in the courtyard of the High Priest just after they had sentenced the Master to death. When I heard their verdict, I was frightened for myself. I was challenged by three people that I was the Lord's disciple. Three times I denied that I even knew him. The Lord had said during our Passover meal that I would, before the cock crowed, deny him three times."

"Well, you didn't knowingly allow the crucifixion of an innocent man."

"Prefect, you didn't know him, I did."

Claudia was sitting on my left. She whispered, "The Lord healed our son. Pilo was born with a turned foot."

Peter smiled. "He healed my mother-in-law too, she was very ill."

Cornelius was listening in and noticed that we weren't eating. "Are you two going to eat?" He said.

***

Peter drained his wine goblet and prepared to speak. He stood and greeted the crowd of fifty people.

I sat back on the lounge and tried to relax. I looked over at Claudia, who was sitting straight up anxiously awaiting Peter's words. I prayed to the gods, *do not let Herod ever hear about this and me being here.*

"I have learned from the Lord in the last few days that he didn't just come for the Jewish people, he came for everyone. That is why I am here. No one is excluded from God's love and mercy."

Peter glanced down at me and repeated his words, "No one is excluded." Our eyes met. I smiled at him. Claudia was smiling too.

Peter spoke at length about Yeshua of Nazareth, in Latin no less. If he was trying to impress me, it was working. He was a powerful speaker. However, my discomfort level wasn't getting any less. I kept glancing at the door, which was guarded by a uniformed Commander Gaius Marius.

As long as Peter keeps speaking, I can't leave.

Peter concluded his remarks by saying, "It is evident to me that the Holy Spirit has come to this household. I see no reason why all of you cannot be baptized into the Lord's church."

"Do we have to become Jewish first?" Cornelius asked.

"No, not at all," Peter replied. "Do you have a pool where I can baptize?"

"Yes, out in the back. Come, everyone," Cornelius said.

Cornelius and his family and guest moved toward the pool area. I hesitated. "Cornelius, I can't. I had better leave."

Peter looked at me. "Another time perhaps?"

"I'm the Emperor's representative in this province, I simply can't."

Peter bowed his head in acknowledgment. He looked at Claudia.

"Husband, may I?" Claudia asked me.

"Yes," I said to her. I was pleased she sought my consent.

"I will see that Lady Claudia is escorted home, sir," Cornelius said.

"Thank you, Cornelius. And thank you for the excellent evening."

"Peter, I am pleased to have met you. May your journeys be safe."

"Peace be with you, Prefect," Peter said.

I started to leave but stopped to watch through the door to the pool as Peter entered the pool followed by Cornelius. Peter plunged Cornelius backward into the water three times declaring, "I baptize you, In the name of the Father, and of the Son, and the Holy Spirit."

There as loud applause from the crowd. Gaius walked by me. "I'm going to be baptized too, sir." He wasn't asking me.

That night my wife and two of my soldiers became followers of what was called "The Way." I couldn't help but feel some responsibility for the rise of this new faith. It seemed to be growing.

One man, a cross, and an empty tomb. How far would it go? Between Caiaphas and Herod, and the intolerance of the empire, which was not to be challenged, I feared for those people, including my family.

49. A Child's Cry

The Palace

I STROLLED TO THE SOUTHWEST PORTICO that faced the sea and the pool. I stared at the spot where I last encountered Yeshua of Nazareth. I never told anyone about it, not even Claudia. It had been three years and the events surrounding that man still reverberated around me. I didn't understand why.

The palace was quiet as the children had been bedded down hours ago by our servants. I poured a cup of wine for myself and went to the worship room. The flame from the prayer cauldron cast a warm glow around the room. Jupiter, our most powerful god and Mars, the god of war, stared at me from their alcoves. I felt nothing for them. I sipped my wine. The goddesses Venus and Juno were there for Claudia though she no longer prayed to them. I felt empty and alone. The worship room seemed pointless, filled with lifeless statues carved out of cold stone. I took another sip of wine.

"I wonder if I should put Yeshua in here. I don't even know how to represent him," I said to myself.

There was another dedicated room in our home. I never entered it. It was Claudia's shrine to a baby born without a breath. The child, a girl, was born six months after our arrival in Caesarea. It was a difficult birth for my wife who never got over delivering the dead child. The cremated remains were held in a jar in a small alcove near the worship room. I stopped at the door. Claudia always left a lamp burning beside the urn. The birth of Pilo helped her recover from the loss of the child, but she never forgot it.

I wish I had asked Yeshua when he was here to… dared I even think that he would do such a thing for me.

A breeze blew around me. I heard a familiar voice. "Ponti" There was only one person who called me by that name. I turned around. There was no one there. The wind encircled me.

"Ponti."

"I hear you, but I cannot see you."

There was fire in the wind that whirled in front of me.

"Know that I am here."

"I can't, you know, get this baptism of yours."

"That's not why I came. There is something you have in your heart that you would like me to do."

"You've read my mind, but it's … it's not for me. It's for my wife. Would you…?"

"Bring me the urn."

I stepped into the shrine and lifted the urn from the shelf where it been for almost ten years. I turned around.

Yeshua, his countenance so brilliant that I could barely look at him, stood in the center of the fire, his hands cupped.

"Pour the ashes into my hands."

My hands trembled as I emptied the contents of the small urn into his hands. I had no doubt he would do the impossible. I stood motionless.

Yeshua blew a gentle breath on the ashes.

The child's cry pierced my ears. I dropped to my knees.

"My child, my child's cry." Claudia's voice rang from the portico. She was quickly at Yeshua's side. He handed the baby to her. She was delirious.

Claudia wrapped the baby in her shawl and spun a glorious dance around the living area and out to the portico, where she proudly showed Cornelius and Gaius our first born. The tears flowed down her beaming face.

When I caught my breath and wiped my own face dry. I looked up to thank Yeshua, but he was gone. The fire and wind had ceased.

Claudia stopped her dancing and sang to the sky, "Thank you, Lord, for restoring my child."

She turned to me.

Claudia placed the child in my arms. "What name do you give her, my husband? Since it is your faith that has brought our daughter back to us, you should name her."

I got up off my knees. "I don't know. Hmm. Should I give her Yeshua's mother's name?"

My wife smiled and said, "That would be beautiful."

"My child, you shall be called Myriam."

Claudia, still reveling in the moment, took Myriam into her arms and began to sing a song to her.

I looked over at Cornelius and Gaius and saw that they too had wet faces. *I guess we Roman soldiers aren't so tough after all.*

"I don't think we have any further use for the worship room," I said. I turned to Cornelius, "Do you think you can help me dispose of it tomorrow? We are going to need another child's room."

"I will be glad to assist you in that effort, sir. What shall we do with the contents?"

I replied, without hesitation, "Throw them into the sea."

I felt the breeze blow around me again.

50. Samaria

Caesarea Maritima

Late Summer

Three years after the Resurrection of Yeshua

THE FREQUENT TRIPS TO JERUSALEM to ensure that peace reigned over the city during feasts and festivals took me away from my other provincial responsibility, Samaria. I depended on the reports from Alexander to keep me informed of any problems that arose in the area.

The Samaritans were Jews but not Temple Jews. The were estranged from the authorities in Jerusalem. They had their own religious practices. They used Mt. Gerizim for their worship place rather than the Temple.

I conscripted my foot soldiers from Samaria. They didn't seem to mind controlling the hordes in Jerusalem. There was a bitter rivalry between the two groups of Jews, which served my purpose well when it came to crowd control. The Emperor had given the Temple Jews the right not to provide service to the army of Rome. In my opinion, the Temple Jewish had far too many privileges granted to them, which made ruling them far more challenging than it needed to be.

Samaria, on the other hand, was far more, shall I say, civil, if that is possible in these parts. Which explains why I only went there twice a year to collect taxes and hear any complaints. When I received word of potential trouble brewing in the area, I was puzzled. I thought, at first, that zealots from Galilee had infiltrated this eastern region of my territory. I soon learned that was not the case.

They had a messiah. The information I had indicated that this messiah was massing an army with the intention of driving out Rome from the land.

"What do we know about this man?" I asked Alexander.

"We don't know his name, sir, but we do know that he claims to be Moses incarnate and that he will show the people the sacred vessels, which they believe Moses buried on Mt. Gerizim and then drive out the Romans."

"How big of an army has he amassed?"

"The number is between a thousand and five thousand men."

"Which is it? That's important to know." I could deal with a thousand but not five thousand. I would have to call for reinforcements from Herod or even Syria. I needed a solid number, and I needed it quickly. I had to act soon.

"Yes, sir. I will get that information."

"Dismissed."

Alexander hurried out of my office. He will no doubt send another spy to Samaria. I poured myself a goblet of wine. The situation worried me. I had not had to suppress any major uprisings in my province since I came here nearly ten years ago. I was not about to allow one to happen in Samaria.

While Alexander's spy gathered the information I needed, I sent word to Commander Marius, who was in Jerusalem for the Summer months, to prepared to bring a thousand troops to Caesarea. I would take another five hundred from here. I had five thousand men at my disposal, but that would mean leaving other parts of Judea unprotected. Not a good plan. We would use Caesarea as a staging ground for what would be an assault on Samaria.

I didn't reveal the uprising to Claudia, as such things troubled her. I certainly did not want her to know I planned to lead the troops myself. The last battle I lead was in northern Gallia over eleven years ago, before our marriage. I swirled the wine in my goblet. The thought of going into battle for the empire roused the old soldier in me. I could not resist.

***

Within five days I had my answer. Alexander's spy had returned with vital information. A thousand armed men were stationed in the village of Tirathana. They were prepared to ascend their sacred mountain, be empowered by this Moses incarnate, then attack Caesarea. I made my decision. I had fifteen hundred troops gathered in Caesarea. I kept them at the garrison out of sight of the palace. I told Claudia that I was going to make a routine administrative trip to Samaria that I would be back in a few days. She did not need to come with me.

"My husband, are you sure you don't need me to come? You know I love the hills of Samaria," Claudia said, trying to worm her way onto the trip.

"No, really, you need to stay here. The children need you." I kissed her. I felt sorry for deceiving her, but it was for the best.

I prayed I would come back alive and never have to tell her about the battle. It occurred to me that I had just prayed to Mars. I wasn't convinced Yeshua would be helpful in combat anyway. He was not that kind of messiah.

I met with Cornelius on my way to join the troops. I told him to keep my reasons for being in Samaria secret from Claudia.

"If, and only if, I don't come back alive, you can tell her the entire story," I advised him.

"Yes, sir. What if the unthinkable happens and you lose the battle, and they head for here, sir? What then?" Cornelius asked.

"You are responsible for the safety of my family. Get them on a ship and take them to Rome. You may not have much time to act. Keep spies on watch far outside the city. They will tell you whether we return or the enemy advances on Caesarea."

"May the Lord be with you, sir," he said.

"Yes, Centurion, I hope so."

51. The Battle

Samaria

HIDING AN ARMY OF FIFTEEN HUNDRED MEN on horses isn't an easy thing to do, not impossible, just difficult. Fortunately, the terrain south and east of Caesarea is mountainous, which creates valleys.

I led the troops through a valley that was obscured by hills. The mountains of the Carmel range provided some cover for our advance on Mt. Gerizim. I was under no illusions that our incursion into Samaria would go unnoticed. No commander of any army would fail to deploy spies on their boundaries. My tactics for securing the area from rebellion did not involve a surprise attack, but strength in numbers and Roman trained men. The best in the world.

I took the route below Mt. Ebal, and in the valley between the two mountains, circled back west and came up of the eastern slopes of Mt. Gerizim. My intention was to block the path up the mountain from the village of Tirathana where the rebels were reportedly stationed.

Half the men came up the mountain trail with me. Commander Marius took remaining troops and circled back around the town. We had them surrounded. But where were they? From my vantage point on the side of the mountain, I could see the village plainly, but I couldn't see any rebel troops, only my own.

Either the reports of the planned rebellion were false or something else was afoot. My steed was antsy. He was as much a battle worn soldier as was I. If he was uneasy...

I heard and felt the thunderous approach of horses, from behind me. I turned. The rebels were on us from above. A sword to sword battle ensued. With only half my troops in the immediate vicinity, we were hopelessly outnumbered.

It was two on one, then three on one. I held my ground. My steed turned and twisted as I evaded direct hits from the swords. I ducked a spear. I knocked two of them off their horses and got a direct hit on the third. The momentary break in direct attacks gave me time to look around. There were more than two thousand rebels against eight hundred of my troops. Commander Marius led the other seven hundred of my men up the mountain. They took up the battle.

I had never seen such combat. Fierce doesn't begin to describe it. I spied what looked like their leader, dressed in gold. I made for him, he didn't see me coming. I drove my spear through the joint in his armor. He fell. Four others came on me. My situation was close to impossible. Marius was at my side. The inexperience of the combatants started to show. Marius and I quickly dispatched the foursome.

The rebels were losing against the better-trained soldiers, just as I had anticipated. It was their numbers that were unexpected. The battle was over. Bodies were strewn over the hillside. Hundreds of rebels, about fifty of my men.

Commander Marius pulled up beside me. "It was a battle for the history books, sir. From where I sat at the edge of the town, there appeared to be three thousand rebels streaming down the mountain toward you."

"Three thousand?"

"Yes, sir."

"Glad, you showed up when you did."

"At your service, sir," Gaius Marius said, as he gave me a salute. I had no doubt of my commander's loyalty.

We marched the remainder of the rebels to the plains of Samaria. Where I gave orders for them to be crucified. Commander Marius came to my side.

"Sir, the majority of these soldiers are not what we would call men. They are mere boys, some as young as my own son."

"What are you suggesting, Commander."

"Let them go."

"Hardly. They will go back and round up more men and attack us in greater numbers."

"Sir, I can't crucify them."

"You…can't…follow…my…orders?"

"No, sir."

I stared at my commander in astonishment. "Get back to the barracks."

"Yes, sir."

I watched him ride away. *Do I kill him or just give him a lashing? One of the two.*

The rest of soldiers carried out their duty as ordered.

We took the bodies of our men back to Caesarea for burial.

I hoped that would be the first and last uprising I would have to put down.

***

The journey back to Caesarea was a mixture of jovial banter among the soldiers who had just won a tough battle and quiet moments of pondering what could have happened. Each man was glad to be alive, myself included.

Commander Marius had made some distance between us. I was boiling. *How dare he.* Marius glanced back at me, with, what I was certain was disgust in his eyes. He shook his head and turned away from me. He kicked his horse to a gallop.

I decided to catch up with him.

"Do you have something to say to me, soldier?"

The commander glanced over his shoulder to see there were no men within earshot. "It was harsh, sir. Just plain harsh. You haven't learned anything from how Yeshua treated you."

"What has this got to with him? Does everything you do have to go through him?"

"It's called mercy, sir. You've got two healthy children thanks to the mercy he has shown you. You could, at least, give it to others."

I was stunned, but I thought it best not to have it out with him. I would wait. "Commander, I will deal with your outburst later."

There was no doubt in my mind that this was insubordination. The only reason I didn't dispatch him then and there was that I owed him my life. I could not have survived the four on one without him.

A few lashes should straighten him out.

***

The bath at the barracks in Caesarea was full. The boisterous soldiers were letting a little steam off after the long ride home. I stood for a moment watching them. I missed the camaraderie of being among the troops. However, it was getting near supper time, but before I joined Claudia in the palace, I had a discipline matter to attend to with Commander Marius.

"Commander, I will see you in the staging room."

He looked up at me and crawled out of the bath. "Yes, sir." He started to put his clothes on.

"You won't need those," I told him as I grabbed a horse whip off the hook in the hallway. The banter in the bath ceased. The soldiers were watching me.

"Sir? What are you going to do?" Marius asked.

"You'll come quietly, or I'll call the others, and you will have an audience."

Marius followed behind me until we got to the door. I opened it and invited him to go in first. I took a torch off the wall, brought it with me and closed the door.

"Commander, what you did out there in the field was insubordination. I should have hung you up."

He was wide-eyed. "Sir. I didn't mean it that way. I…"

"Enough! Turn around. Hands up against the wall."

He's lucky this is just a horse whip. I could see him stiffen. He was saying something under his breath.

"What are you doing Marius?"

"Praying, sir. It's called the Lord's Prayer. Yeshua gave it to us. I've just got to part that goes like this, *'forgive us our sins as we forgive those who have sinned against us and deliver us from evil.'…."*

"Stop. Stop it right now."

"Yes, sir."

He threw me off. I lost my focus. I stood there for a few minutes staring at the whip in my hand. *He doesn't deserve this. Yeshua didn't deserve it either.*

"Take your hands down, Commander."

"Thank you, sir."

I moved in right behind him. "This is as close to mercy as you'll get from me. Got it?" I said in his ear.

"Yes, sir."

Just then the door opened. It was Cornelius.

"The soldiers told me I would find you two here. What is going on?"

Cornelius took the whip out of my hand. "Is this the way you treat the man who, by all account, saved your life?"

"We just had a discussion about mercy."

"Really? Because, sir, you are going to need some. Your wife has heard about the real reason for your trip to Samaria, and she is not happy."

"She has her father's temper," I replied.

"Oh, and where did you get yours, sir?" Cornelius said.

"Are you both going to be insubordinate today? What is this, a contest?"

"No, sir, just two friends trying to get you to see the light," Gaius countered.

By the time I got to the door, I was laughing. "The light? What is the light?"

"The same thing as the truth, sir," Gaius replied. "And you know the answer to that question."

"That's enough soldier. I'm done here."

"Come, Cornelius, if I'm going to encounter my wife I had better have my bodyguard with me."

"I'm off duty, sir. You are on your own."

"Gaius?"

"I need to finish my bath, sir."

"Traitors."

52. An Order from Syria

Caesarea Maritima

I T TOOK A FEW DAYS, NO MAKE THAT A FEW WEEKS before Claudia let me back in the marriage bed. She called me a few names like *stupid, war monger, and a liar,* but the one that stung the most was *old man.* What I didn't admit to her was that she was right.

I spent many hours getting a massage for my painful right arm and my back. It turned out I was not in shape to go into battle. Nine years of being a provincial administrator had softened me up. I was closing in on forty, and I felt it.

During my convalescence, I sent a letter to Tiberius to advise him about the planned Samaritan uprising and how my troops though outnumbered, were victorious. I dispatched the letter at the end of September before the winter significantly restricted sea travel because of rough waters.

We spent winters in Caesarea where the climate was moderate and usually free of snow that sometimes fell in Jerusalem and in the mountains. Our first journey in the early spring was to Jerusalem for Passover. The majority of troops, also over wintered in Caesarea and returned to Jerusalem with us.

We had just returned from Jerusalem in April of my tenth year as Prefect when the authority of Rome descended on me and my household.

I can't help but remember every painful detail of my final day in office as Prefect of Judea, Samaria, and Idumea. The day was full of administrative duties with barely enough time to have a meal with Claudia and the children. It was late afternoon when I heard and felt the thunderous approach of horses. I thought it was strange because I hadn't called for any troops. I walked to the portico. The noise came from the north side of the palace.

Soldiers. There must have been close to fifty men on horseback. They were riding under the banner of the Legat of Syria. As they got closer, I saw who led them, Marcus Rufus, my former commander.

It suddenly occurred to me, they were coming for me.

"Claudia!" I called, "get the children." She came out carrying Myriam with little Claudia in tow. She ran back in to get Pilo. He was downstairs in the paddock, grooming his steed.

Rufus came up the stairs holding a sealed scroll in his hands. He offered me no salute. He said nothing as he handed the scroll to me. It had the seal of Tiberius Caesar on it. I opened it. I read the inscription.

Pontius Pilate is charged with mass murder against the people of Samaria and is ordered to appear in Rome immediately to face trial by Tiberius Caesar. This order is given by Lucius Vitellius, Legat of Syria.

"Mass murder?" I was astonished. "It was a revolt."

"You'll have to make that plea to the Emperor," Rufus said. He was stone-faced, but I could see the satisfaction in his eyes.

"Your family has until tomorrow morning to ready themselves for travel. You are to be held in the prison overnight. Tomorrow morning all of you will board the ship for Rome," Rufus said.

"May I speak with my wife?"

He nodded.

Claudia and Pilo watched from inside. They came out so I could speak to them. "Claudia, gather what you can for the voyage. There's a long box in the wine cellar. If it is too difficult to bring, hide it somewhere."

Claudia was shaking and close to tears. "What's in it?"

"Scrolls. I can't tell you what they contain, at least not now."

I gave her a hug and motioned to Pilo. He was terrified. I kissed him, "Be brave Pilo, I need you to take care of your mother and your sisters."

I ran my fingers down little Claudia's face.

"Tata," she said.

I kissed Myriam.

Centurion Cornelius and Commander Marius came to the portico. Marius was brandishing his sword. I shook my head at him. He sheathed it.

Rufus stripped me of the medallions of my office as Prefect and pulled the ring of my office off my right ring finger. He threw it on the stone floor and smashed it with his heel.

He ordered me to put my hands behind my back. I was officially a prisoner of Rome. The only thing that would save me from crucifixion was my Roman citizenship.

"Guards, take him to the prison," Rufus ordered.

The Syrian soldiers hauled me to my own dungeon for the night. Why they sent fifty men to arrest me, I have no idea, unless the stories of my performance during battles made them think I could take on the Roman army single-handily. I smiled at the thought. I was good in battle, but not that good.

As I was dragged down the stairs to the prison cell, I saw Rufus whisper something to one of his men. I wondered how I would survive what was about to happen. The clanging of the cell door snapped me out of my thoughts. I was now the former prefect. If I had any illusions of being treated differently than any criminal; those thoughts disappeared as the soldiers threw me to the floor. They were about to have some fun with me.

The door of the prison slammed shut. It was dark. There were, at least, three soldiers in the cell with me. I felt a boot hit my left leg. It wasn't a hard hit. One of them grabbed me, pulled me to my feet and punched me in the face. He dropped me, and the kicking began in earnest.

My stomach got it first. Then my back, my head, and my face, they didn't miss any part of me. The pain seared through my back. I vomited. I could hardly breathe. Finally, they stopped. I was expected to arrive in Rome alive.

I heard a thud from the door. The soldiers were gone. They had done Rufus' work.

I laid on the floor in terrible pain. I was sure something was broken. I couldn't stretch out. I curled up in a ball. It was the only position that felt even slightly comfortable. Sometime during the night, I fell into a restless sleep.

***

The noise of the prison door opening woke me. Someone sat me up. I couldn't see who because my eyes were swollen shut. A cup was put to my lips. I drank the water. A cold, wet cloth was pressed against my eyes.

"I'll stay with you. I will see to it nothing further happens to you. However, you must do exactly as I say. Do you understand?"

"Yes, Commander, I do?"

"I will ensure your safety. You must trust me," Commander Marius said.

"What about my family? Is Cornelius going with them?"

"No. He has to stay here. A new Prefect is coming today from Alexandria. I will keep watch on your family too, sir."

"Does Rufus know you are doing this?"

"As far as Rufus is concerned, he thinks I'm going to ensure you don't die en route, which tends to happen to prisoners."

Gaius had breakfast for me. He gave me a piece of bread, but my hand shook so much I couldn't hold it. He held it to my mouth. I was able to eat some of it and the cheese he gave me. My stomach was starting to feel better.

I leaned against Gaius as he lifted me to my feet. My legs nearly gave out from under me. They were sore from the beating. Gaius helped me walk around the small prison space. It was enough to get my stiff muscles to move. The swelling of my eyes made it difficult to see.

"Can you walk on your own?"

"I'll try, " I replied. I could walk, but just barely.

"I have to put these chains on your feet and hands. Sorry."

He latched the metal cuffs to my ankles and wrists. I swallowed hard. The seriousness of my situation was sinking in. Never, did I expect to be leaving my province in chains. *Maybe it would be better to die on the ship.*

***

"Bring the prisoner," Rufus called from above.

Gaius took me by my arm and helped me up the stairs. The sunlight struck my eyes. I couldn't see.

"This way, sir," he said.

"You don't have to call me that anymore. I'm not commanding you now and since we are going to be on board a ship for the next three weeks, you can all me Pontius."

"Fine, Pontius, sir."

"It hurts to laugh, Gaius."

"I'll try not to be funny, sir," he said with a grin on his face.

My eyes were adjusting to the light, and the swelling had eased. We walked to the ship. It was a commercial ship. Which meant we would be onboard with travelers and merchants. I would be put in the cargo hold. We walked down the lower plank. The captain met us as we boarded. He checked the papers Gaius was carrying.

"Take him to the bow of the ship. There is hold there with a lock on it. We use that for the likes of him. Pontius Pilate, welcome aboard," he said as he feigned a bow. He gave Gaius a set of keys.

Gaius led me through the stacks of cargo and grain bound for Italia. The stench was terrible, I tried to hold my breath, but that was pointless. The only light in the hold came through the grates in the deck above us. I looked up and wondered if Claudia and the children had boarded yet.

"Is my family on board?"

"Yes, they would have boarded an hour ago. We are the last on the ship. I will check them once we are under sail," Gaius replied.

"Thank you."

He took me to the small hold at the bow. It was no more four feet by six feet. That was where I would spend the next twenty-one days if the wind is favorable. There was a chain on the floor. Rats scurried out of the hold when we entered. Gaius unhooked the chain from the shackles on my leg and attached the floor chain. He took the cuffs off my hands.

"Won't need those. You aren't going anywhere."

Gaius unpacked a bag he had be carrying. He put several blankets and a cushion on the floor. "It gets cold down here."

"Thank you."

"I'll be right back, I'm going to get some water"""

Gaius closed the door and locked it. He opened a pass through window. It let some light into my small dungeon. I sat down on the blankets and leaned back against the hull. *My life is over.*

***

"I'm back," Gaius said as he unlocked the door.

He set the bucket of water with a scoop in it on the floor. He put a second empty bucket at the back corner of the cell. I knew what that was for.

"Thanks, again, Gaius."

"Your welcome, sir. We'll be heading out to sea soon. The tide is in.The ship is going to Alexandria first then to Rome. I'll be right outside your door. Call me if you need anything."

"I will."

I heard the ship's anchor being lifted. The ship lurched. We had left the port of Caesarea Maritima. I remembered how beautiful the city looked from the ship when we arrived. The gleaming white buildings and the palace near the shore had both Claudia and me excited. I could see no such sight now. I buried my head in my hands. I could not longer control my emotions. *I wish those soldiers had killed me.*

53. Prisoner

S EASICKNESS HAD ME IN ITS GRIP. Gaius did his best to keep me from passing out. I could keep neither food or water down. I was sick on the way to Judea but only for a few days. This bout hadn't let up.

Gaius delivered notes from my family. They said they were well. Pilo wrote that he was strong and was looking after his mother and his sisters, just as I had asked him. I had no doubt that Pilo was becoming a man at ten because of this terrible journey that I had caused my family.

I did not know whether it was day or night. If Gaius brought me food, I figured it was day, if he was snoring, it was night. When I wasn't too sick, he would take me for a walk along the length of the ship so I wouldn't lose the use of my legs.

Every day I would ask Gaius the same question, "How many days to Rome?" His answer was always one day less than the day before. That's how I knew that we were more than halfway through the voyage when Gaius got permission to take me topside. I was grateful. I had hopes of seeing my family.

Gaius unshackled my leg from the hull of the ship. He took the handcuffs and put one on himself and the other on me, chaining us together. We ascended the ladder, he went first.

"Cover your eyes. The light will hurt," he told me. When we reached the deck, I let the light in my eyes by lifting one finger at a time. It was still too bright, so I took short blinks until they adjusted.

Gaius led me to the ship's side rail. He took the cuff off his wrist and attached it to the rail. I was finally able to look out on the blue-green waters of Mare Nostrum. I took my first breath of fresh air in two weeks. The sky was bright blue with a few white wisp of clouds. The wind blew gently against the sails. A mariner's perfect day.

I was glad to get out. They didn't let me up during the stop at Alexandria. It occurred to me that we were the only ones on deck. "Where is everyone?" I asked.

"They are on the port side. You are not permitted to mix with the passengers, including your family. I know you were hoping to see them. The captain wouldn't allow it. I'm sorry."

My heart sank. He was right. I had hoped to see them. I just didn't dare ask.

"Where are we?" I queried to change the subject for my own benefit.

"In the middle of the sea, a week away from Rome. I'm going down to the galley to get us some lunch. Don't try and jump ship."

"I wouldn't think of it."

***

Gaius returned with a pile of food on one plate.

"How many are you feeding?"

"Just us," he said. He portioned it in half and handed me the plate. I looked at the food and then at Gaius. "Have you been giving me half of your food?"

"You'd never survive on the amount of food assign to a prisoner," he replied.

"Gaius."

"I'm doing as well as are you. So, eat your half and then I'll eat mine."

I downed my portion and then handed the plate back to him.

I glanced at the sea. It seemed so peaceful. I was not. Rome and my death were only a week away.

"You know, Gaius, I would normally be excited about returning to Rome, but now, I'm terrified. I don't even know why I'm admitting this to you."

He put his plate down and wiped his face on his sleeve, reminding me of Pilo.

"It's understandable, sir."

"I don't even know why I'm being charged. I mean, there was a rebellion. They attacked us. We defended ourselves. And, unless the policies of the emperor have changed, I put to death those who attacked us and plotted against Rome." I shook my head. "I just don't understand."

"Politics."

"How could that be it? If Tiberius wanted me out of there, all he had to do was end my term. No, there's something else going on."

"Vitellius. He is replacing you with one of his good friends. I heard from Rufus that the Samaritans complained, and that was all he needed to recommend the charge to get you out of there. Tiberius agreed."

"So, that's what happened."

"I think so, sir. That's about as much as I know. There was a complaint about the battle."

"So, when I go before Tiberius it will be my word against the Samaritans. Tiberius has received complaints about me from the Sanhedrin for years, this one was probably the last straw."

I leaned against the railing and stared out at the sea. "It's hopeless."

I thought for a moment. The waves of the sea rhythmically pushed up against the side of the boat. I look toward the bow as it cut through the water.

I had a flashback, I saw the water splashing on my hands as I tried to wash them free of Yeshua's blood.

"Gaius, what was that prayer you said Yeshua gave you? You know, the one you said when I was threatening you with the whip. "

I threaten to lash my good friend with a whip. What kind of man am I?

"The Lord's Prayer."

"I think I need it. Will you teach it to me or better still, write it down?"

"I sure will. Just a minute, I'll get something to write on." He disappeared down the stairs.

Maybe it's too late for me. I should have accepted the baptism from Peter when he offered it.

Gaius was back and writing on a scroll. He finished and handed it to me. I read it. "Pater noster, qui es in cælis, nomen sanctum…

"I thought this was a prayer to Yeshua, why does it start with *Pater Noster*? Who is that?

"I guess I should start at the beginning of Jewish scriptures. I grew up in Galilee so their stories are familiar to me. You know about the Exodus story being Passover."

"Yes, sort of."

"Well before that….long before that. There was this story of God as creator and, according to Yeshua, Father of all. It goes like this, *In the beginning…*"

I had to smile as this Roman soldier sat there and recounted the Jewish Book of Genesis in its entirety. I was getting a little tired when he got to Abraham, but I listened anyway. It was interesting, to say the least. But then, I had to stop him.

"Wait a minute, did you just say the God told Abraham to sacrifice his own son?"

"Yes, but there's more."

Just as he was about to continue the ship's captain came. "It's time to get the prisoner back in the hold."

Gaius unhooked my hand from the railing and led me downstairs back to my cell. The stench from the lower deck hit me in the face. I started choking. I couldn't believe I'd been living in that filth for two weeks and one more to go.

I stretched out on my blanket and stared into the blackness. The ship rocked back and forth. I felt the bow lift more than usual. A storm was brewing. The ship creaked. I heard the covers going on the portals in the deck. The ship lurched and rolled. Cargo crashed to the floor.

"Gaius are you alright out there?"

"Yes, some pieces of the shipment might not be, though."

I heard muffled shouts above me. Orders were being given. The bow lurched again. Higher this time. The storm was getting dangerous.

"Do you think my family will be safe, Gaius?"

"I'll go up and check as soon as it evens out. I couldn't stand on the stairs right now. But I'm sure the passengers are well protected from such storms."

"Thanks."

My stomach started to feel queasy. I grabbed the empty bucket. I was sick again. The storm lasted most of the night. The rocking of the ship eventually put me to sleep

Yeshua's prayer stayed with me. I woke through the night, it was there. I repeated it in my head. I found it strangely comforting. *Abraham was asked to give up his son. I wanted to hear the rest of the story.*

***

Gaius attended to me like a mother hen, especially when we were in port. His story telling didn't let up. I knew he was trying to keep my mind off my impending doom at the hands of the Emperor, but it got to the point where I could no longer listen to his words. I didn't have the luxury of contemplating the words of prophets, kings or even Yeshua for that matter.

I desperately wanted to get off the ship at any dock, except Rome's. I needed to see my family, one last time.

"Gaius, I hate to interrupt the words of Isaiah, but do you think that before we go ashore in Rome, that I could see my family."

He could see my anxiety. He reached out and put his hand on my shoulder. "I will ask, again."

Gaius locked my door. I heard his heavy footsteps go up the ladder. I had become familiar with the sound of his departures, and his returns. I sat back against the hull and waited.

***

I heard footsteps on the ladder, they were light steps, a couple of sets of light steps, I was sure. They were followed by Gaius' familiar thud on the steps. I got up. I heard a whispered voice – Claudia's voice.

"Which way, Gaius? I can't see anything?"

"To your right. Here, give me your hand. Pilo can you make your way?"

"Yes, I can see a little. It smells bad down here."

"Hold your nose, dear."

"He's over here. I'll open his door. Sir, I have visitors for you."

My emotions caught me. I could hardly speak. Pilo was first in the door. He wrapped himself around my waist.

"Pater, Pater," he cried.

I couldn't speak. I hugged him tight. Claudia held both of us in her arms. I lifted my face to hers. We kissed. I put my head on her shoulder.

I heard a little voice. "Tata?" I saw Claudia standing by Gaius, I knelt to be at her level. I found my voice. "Sweetheart, come give Tata a hug." She kissed my face and hung herself around my neck. I held her close.

"Don't worry, Tata, Mater asked Yeshua to help you. We believe he will."

"I hope so dear one," I told her even though I wasn't sure. What could he do?

Gaius was holding Myriam. I took her from him. She slept with her head on my shoulder. I kissed her forehead. At only three there's a chance she will not remember me. She would grow up never knowing her father. I gave her to Claudia.

"They can't stay long, sir. The captain said he is breaking the rules letting this happen, so I have to take them back up immediately," Gaius said.

"Tell him I said "thank you.""

I embraced Gaius. I had no words to express my gratitude. He nodded. He understood.

My family filed out of my little prison. I held on to Claudia as long as I could. She stepped out of my reach.

"Bye, Tata," Little Claudia said.

Gaius closed the door and locked it.

54. Rome

March 18, [37 A.D.]

The Port of Ostia (Rome)

THE SHIP LURCHED AND THEN SETTLED TO A STOP as it landed portside at Portus Ostia, the home port for land-bound Rome. It was the busiest port in the empire. All ships travel to Rome, eventually. The empire was a hungry beast. And I was about to get fed to it.

My heart thumped hard in my chest, there was a pain in my stomach. I laid on the floor and waited, Gaius would call me when he was ready to transfer me to a court official at dockside. Surrounded by darkness and rank air for twenty-one days, I wasn't in a fighting mood. I don't think I could have argued for my life; I no longer had it in me. The executioner's blade would almost be a welcome relief. These were the darkest hours of my life. *I would most likely be hauled off to prison tonight, go before Tiberius in the morning and be executed before noon.*

Those thoughts turned over and over in my mind. The only comfort I had was that the charge wasn't treason so my family would be spared. Besides, I couldn't believe Tiberius would kill his own daughter and grandchildren. But, it was known that he starved Claudia's mother to death. He then gave a home to Claudia.

Please, Yeshua, keep my family safe. I ask nothing for myself only for them.

I heard and felt a loud thump. I caught a whiff of fresh sea air. The cargo door of the ship was open. It was time. Gaius unlocked the door.

"You can come now, sir. All the other passengers are off. We will exit through the back portal, the same way we came in."

I slipped passed Gaius, as I did, he pulled his arm across his chest and snapped his heels together. I looked at him and smiled. "Thank you, Tribune." I returned his salute.

***

I shuffled to the cargo port. The gangplank was even with the dock. Gaius had hold of my arm as I moved my chained feet along it. I had to be careful not to trip. When I got half way to the dock I looked up and saw what I expected, an official from the court.

"Pontius Pilate?" he asked.

"Yes."

"The gods are smiling on you today," he said.

I was confused. "Smiling?"

"Tiberius Caesar is dead two days now. Emperor Claudius has stayed the charges against all those who are accused of a crime under the late Emperor. You are free to go to your home until your case is reviewed by the Emperor. Be ready at any time to be summoned to the court. You must not leave Rome. Do you understand?"

"I do," I said. I was stunned.

"Tribune, you may release the prisoner."

Gaius retrieved the key for my cuffs and chains on my feet. He freed me. Gaius put his arm around my shoulder and pointed up the dock. "Your family, sir. Go to them."

I held my emotions in and went to meet my wife and children. We met halfway. I held Claudia in my arms. She was in tears.

"I have you, but my father is dead." It was hard for her. I pulled her closer to me.

"Let's gather our baggage, hire a cart and go home. We've been through a lot."

Claudia nodded in silence. Pilo reached out to me. I threw my arms around him and little Claudia. It occurred to me that my children had never seen Rome. In their short lives, Judea had been their only home.

"We are going to live in the place where I grew up. You will like it. There is lots of space and a paddock." I told them.

"Will I have a steed, Pater?" Pilo asked.

"I want a steed too," little Claudia piped in.

"Yes, my children, yes."

Gaius retrieved the few bags Claudia had managed to pack before we left Caesarea. I checked them, one item I expected to see wasn't there.

"The box with the scrolls – you couldn't bring it?" I asked her.

"No, but Cornelius took it. He said he would put it with the other item he had. The one, he said, you ordered him to destroy. He would not reveal to me what it was or what is on the scrolls. Are you going to tell me?"

I smiled. "I will dear. For now, let's go home."

Gaius ordered a cart with horse and driver for us. I helped him put the four bags on the cart. The children climbed on. I held Myriam while Claudia situated herself next to Pilo. I sat beside him. Little Claudia sat next to her mother. Gaius sat next to the driver.

The children were wide-eyed as we made our way through Rome. The Ponti Villa was on the northside of the city. I still had a couple of servants working there to keep the place functional. I never knew how long I would be in Judea. It had been ten years, and they didn't know we were coming.

I still felt uneasy. I wasn't completely free. There would be the review of the charge in front of Caligula or Claudius as he preferred to be called. The new emperor was an unpredictable man known for his unexpected outbursts and violence even toward his friends. He was Claudia's cousin. I didn't know how that would situate us with him. I remembered what Cornelius had said to me about Pilo being in line for the throne because he was the great-grandson of Augustus. I held Pilo close and shook my head. *Not possible.*

The city of Rome hadn't changed much in ten years, except it was much busier. I watched Pilo as he took in the sights, smells and sounds of the greatest city on earth. Here, he would become a true Roman.

"Where does the Emperor live Pater?"

"In a palace in the center of the city near the river. We won't be going that way today, I'll take you someday."

The ride to our villa took just under an hour from the port. The villa was on a private road surrounded by fields and orchards. I never looked after the grounds we always had servants for that.

As we pulled up to the front door, Claudia looked over her shoulder at our home, a low rise building with family and guest wings at either end. We had only spent a few months there after our marriage. We would both need to get reacquainted with it.

"The first thing I'm going to do is get into the bath," I told her.

"That's good," she replied. She giggled.

"I know, I know, I stink."

My servants must have heard us coming; they were out the door and attending to the children and our baggage.

***

The bath, located at the back of the villa, was fed by a natural hot spring. It wasn't a large pool but was suitable for ten men on one side and five women on the other side. Gaius and I relaxed in its soothing warmth. Claudia was being attended by her servant girl. A curtain separated the two sides so we could still carry on a conversation.

"I resigned my posting in Judea before I left," Gaius said.

"Why?"I asked him.

"I was told that the incoming prefect was bringing his own Tribune, so I figured it would be best to move on."

"What are you going to do?"

"There's a small but growing community of the Lord's followers here in Rome, so I thought I would join them and help out. I plan to send for my family as soon as I can find a place and get settled."

"Would you still serve as a soldier?"

"No, I plan to leave the army in the next few weeks."

"You were born in Galilee weren't you, Gaius? It's your home." Claudia chimed in.

"Yes, but I want to play a greater role in the Lord's mission. The apostles and many of his disciples are going to all parts of the earth just as he told them."

I shook my head, "And Caiaphas thought that by killing Yeshua it would put an end to his words. It has done the opposite."

"The church is growing all over the empire in some places openly, in other places underground, like here in Rome. Simon Peter is here."

"Is he? Are you planning to meet with him again?"

"Yes, in a few days. Would you like me to bring him here?"

"Yes," Claudia said,

"I don't think that would be wise just now. Claudius might have his spies watching us – or me for that matter. It might not be safe for Peter." I replied.

I wasn't sure if I was safe.

There was one person I wanted to see, my old friend Seneca. He was one person I could engage in a philosophical discussion, a passion of my youth before the army and battles got in the way.

55. The Philosopher

The Ponti Estate

Rome

W E SETTLED INTO OUR HOME with relative ease. At least the walls and landscape suited us. I had one primary concern. Money. I was forced to leave Caesarea with only the toga I was wearing, which Claudia deemed too filthy to even consider worth washing. She burned it. I had left nothing behind at the villa when we went to Judea, so I had to borrow clothing from my servant.

Claudia brought the essential clothing for herself and the children. She never thought to grab what money we had in the palace. I hadn't been paid for my last month of service, and because I had a pending charge, I would not be paid unless it was dropped

When we arrived, our servants had some food in the villa store room, such as flour for bread, fruit from the orchard, vegetables, and some salted fish. We used to have chickens, but I gave up trying to keep them years ago. So, I had a full house with food running low. I couldn't even pay my servants. They used to be slaves, but my father freed them before his death. They wanted to stay on with us not as slaves but as workers. I owed them wages.

Gaius moved to a community of Yeshua's disciples within a week of our arrival so as not to burden us with another adult to feed. It troubled me that he had to do that because of the care he showed me during the voyage.

A couple of days after he had gone to the community, Gaius and several other members arrived at our door with a cart full of food, enough to last a month. We were a little embarrassed but grateful.

The gift of food couldn't have arrived at a better time. The following day, my friend Lucius Annaeus Seneca came for a visit. He had heard of my return from Judea and was concerned about the circumstances.

Seneca was well known in the academic circles of Rome, following in his father's footsteps, he was deeply engaged in the philosophies of the Greeks and the Romans. I always found him a profound and engaging conversationalist. Indeed his visit was an excellent opportunity to get my mind off my current circumstances, at least that's what I had expected.

"Welcome home my friend," Seneca said in greeting. "I have brought you some of the finest wine from Gallia."

"Thank you, Seneca. It is wonderful to see you at long last," I replied.

He greeted Claudia, who introduced him to our children. My family departed to other parts of the house leaving Seneca and me to get caught up.

My servant poured two goblets of wine and handed them to us while we settled on the lounges near the pool at the back of the villa. The afternoon sun sparkled off the water. I felt relaxed.

"So, Pilate tell me why you have arrived back from you posting facing a charge of mass murder? I know you tend to be short-tempered and abrupt, but mass murder? That's quite the charge even for you. What did you do?"

I took at gulp of wine. I wasn't quite expecting that as a conversation opener, but my friend deserved an answer.

"There was a planned revolt in Samaria. I rallied the troops. There was a battle, we won, and I put the surviving enemy men to death. The Samaritans complained to Vitellius, the Legate of Syria about it, so here I am."

Seneca shook his head. "I doubt you'll have much of a problem getting the emperor to drop the charge. Tiberius was soft on the Jews and their rebellious nature, but Claudius will most probably shrug it off."

"That's good to hear. I wasn't sure how I would stand with him."

"Listen there's another reason I'm interested in hearing about what happened in Judea while you were there," Seneca said as he leaned in closer to me and lowered his voice.

"I've had the opportunity to listen to a fiery Jewish preacher from Tarsus, I believe his name was Paul. He had quite the story to tell about a man who was condemned to crucifixion by you and rose from the dead. Is this true? Do you know anything about this man? I believe his name was Iesus. Paul also called him by the title Christos.

I polished off my wine and held the goblet out to my servant for another filling.

"Yes, Seneca, it is all true."

"Paul said this Iesus is the Son of God, the Jews' God. Did you know that when you condemned him?"

"It was suggested to me by the Sanhedrin, that he made such a claim, but that didn't concern me. It was against their religion that's why they brought him to me."

"Why did you have him crucified?"

"I was told he claimed to be the 'King of the Jews.' That was an affront against the emperor."

"I see." Seneca rubbed his chin, as philosophers do when they are thinking.

"You said that it was 'all true' about this man Iesus, does that include rising from the dead?"

"Yes, he surely did."

"How do you know this with such certainty?"

I drained my goblet again and held it out for more. *This wine is good.*

"I saw him three times after his death. I do have good reason to believe in his divinity."

"Tell me.."

The excellent wine from Gallia was starting to go to my head.

"My family."

"What about them?"

"Do you remember what I told you about Pilo when he was born? That he had a crippled foot?"

"Yes, I do remember, you feared he would never walk."

"What did you see when Claudia introduced you to him."

"He stood tall and straight. Did the physicians fix his foot?"

"No, Iesus did during the trial while I was out in the Pavement taking to the High Priest. I didn't notice until the next day. The man I sent to the cross healed my son. Really shook me."

"So, what happened?"

"Sunday morning. I got word that his tomb was empty and.that his body was stolen. However, the centurion reported that while he was guarding the tomb, Yeshua, that's his Jewish name, came out of the grave. A few days later, on our way back to Caesarea, I saw him myself."

"His ghost?"

"At first, I thought so, but days later I met him again and touched him He was physically alive."

"Are sure he died? Perhaps he came to in the grave. It can happen."

"The centurion ran his sword through to his heart."

"The same soldier who witnessed the so-called resurrection?"

"Yes. There is more. It will take another visit and more wine for me to tell you the whole story.

"That would be excellent. So, tell me. Do you worship him?"

"I pray to him. I threw the Roman gods into the sea."

"Oh, Pilate no! If Claudius gets wind of that you had better get out Rome while you still have your life."

I took a sip of wine. "I'll take your words of wisdom under advisement. But if he asks me, I will tell the truth."

"I'll wait for the rest of your story about this man."

"As a philosopher, I think you will not only be interested in what Iesus did but also what he said."

"You have piqued my interest, but I must take my leave."

"There is one more thing you should know. You saw our youngest child, Myriam?"

"Yes."

"She is our first born. She was born dead a few months after our arrival in Caesarea."

"What?"

"Claudia kept her ashes in an urn. Yeshua came one evening and restored her life to us. I named her after his mother. I'll give you the details later."

Seneca's mouth was wide open. I finished my wine.

"Fine, Pontius, fine. Enough with your drunken stories. Now, I know you're pulling my leg."

He got off the lounge and headed for the door. I followed him. He turned briefly in my direction. "Let me know how you make out with the Emperor and don't tell him that story, he'll put you in a special room with no windows."

"But it's true…" I started to say, but my friend was out the door. I realized that if he didn't believe me, who would?

56. Summoned

Two Months Later

M Y WIFE IS MUCH MORE SELF-RELIANT than I am. I've always been waited on while at home or served by the lower ranking soldiers in the field. In the two months since coming back to Rome, Claudia had managed to make her own preserves from the orchard and sell them in the marketplace. They sold well. We had an income. Life was getting comfortable again. Yeshua's followers, who called themselves Christians, still helped us when they could. Claudia made sure it was a fair exchange of goods or services.

The time crept on for me. I wanted my life back the way it was. I needed to work. Being practically imprisoned in my own home was getting to me.

Summer was in full force in Italia. It was hot and dry. The orchards weren't doing well. Just when we thought we were finally getting back to some normalcy, our source of income was drying up in the heat of Summer.

***

Claudia had put the girls down for an afternoon nap before she joined Pilo and me at the pool. We sat in the shade and enjoyed some fruit drinks.

Claudia was uneasy. She got up from her lounge and walked to the gate at the side of the house. She turned around and started pacing.

"I'm not feeling well," she said.

"Are you ill, my dear?"

She returned to her lounge. "No. I have a feeling in the pit of my stomach that something bad is going to happen."

I put my arm around her. Her face was bleached white, her eyes were large and fixed in a stare. Her breathing was slow, and her mouth was tensed.

"Pater, what's wrong with Mater? Pilo asked.

"She is having a spell. She'll be well again soon." I told him, not entirely convinced of my own words.

Claudia fell back into my arms in a faint. Tears poured down her face. I was certain something terrible was happening in her dream or vision, whatever it was.

I heard a loud knock on the front door. I called for my servant to answer it. I had Claudia in my arms. She was still in her faint.

"Claudia, wake up dear," I said as I splashed some water on her face. "Claudia?"

"Pater?" Pilo said.

"She'll be alright, Pilo, I said without looking up.

"Pilate, I need to speak to you, the Emperor summons you."

Startled by the strange male voice. I looked to see the court official standing by Pilo.

"He summons you along with your wife and son."

Claudia started to come out of her faint. She sat up and stared at the official. I felt her shaking.

"My wife is ill and my son? Why my son?"

"I have my orders. You, your wife and son are to come with me immediately."

He didn't need to say another word, he pulled back his cloak to show me his sword. If we refused to go, he had orders to kill us.

57. The Court of Claudius

Emperor's Palace

Rome

MY HUSBAND HELPED ME TO MY FEET, Pilo held my arm, between them I managed to walk to the waiting carriage. The horrible vision was frozen in my mind. I knew what was going to happen. I had only one hope, one prayer, *Lord help us.*

Pontius held me close and kissed my head. He knew as well as I what was coming. Pilo sat next to his father. Stunned and frighten, my brave boy wiped his face on his sleeve.

The girls what would happen to them? We left them at the villa, sleeping. They were not in the vision. My children, my children.

The carriage pulled up to the palace, the place where I spent ten years after my mother died. Tiberius took me in, as his niece, but everyone suspected he was my father.

We were hauled out of the carriage. Bindings were slapped around our wrist. Pontius glanced at me. His face was grave.

We walked the long ornate hallway to the throne room. We said nothing between us. Pilo tried not to cry. My heart ached for him.

We turned in front of the doors to the throne room. The court official went inside while we waited with two soldiers on either side of us. The door opened, we were called forward.

He was a sight to behold. Caligula, as he was once called, now held the authority over our lives. I had never seen an emperor so clothed in gold as I saw sitting on the throne that day.

The Emperor stood and walked toward us. He set his gaze on Pontius.

"Pontius Pilate, I have examined the charge of mass murder brought against you by the late Tiberius Caesar, and I have determined that you are guilty as charged. You are sentenced to be executed forthwith."

My husband's pallor went gray. He swayed like a leaf in the wind. I couldn't breathe. I knew the pronunciations weren't over. Emperor Claudius turned to me.

"Claudia, I see that the years in Judea have not changed your beauty one bit. It is unfortunate for you and your son that you are my cousins." He gave me a sneer. I didn't understand where he was going.

"You should know that I can't abide that there is another line of succession from Augustus other than mine." He ran his hand down the side of Pilo's face. My stomach churned. *Lord help us*! Again, I pleaded.

"Take all of them to the executioner."

That was it. We were pushed out of the throne room down a long narrow hall. I looked over my shoulder at Pontius. He shook his head.

"Cornelius warned me about this, I thought he was just making it up. I am so sorry, Claudia."

"It's not your fault."

"He doesn't know about our daughters. I pray they will be saved by our servants."

We continued downward into a dark tunnel. Then, I saw the executioner. We stopped in front of him. The tunnel continued beyond where we stood. It turned into a chute from which our bodies would be pushed down into the river.

The soldier, who had brought us to him, handed the executioner the emperor's orders.

"Pontius Pilate, come forward and kneel facing the chute."

Pontius looked at Pilo and me and mouthed "I love you both." He knelt next to the executioner's feet and started to pray the Lord's Prayer. Pilo and I joined him. We too prayed.

I saw the glint from the sword as it was lifted over our heads.

A light, the brightest light I'd ever seen, filled the tunnel. The executioner screamed. His sword clattered to the ground. The soldier tumbled. My bindings fell off. Then a voice came from the light.

"Go, Ponti, take your family down the chute and swim for your lives."

Pontius and Pilo were free. Pontius grabbed Pilo and put him in my arms. He pushed us both down the chute. He jumped down behind us.

The water stung as I hit it. I lost my grip on Pilo. "Swim Pilo, swim," I called out to him,

"Mater, I'm over here.".

There was a big splash in the water, Pontius was with us. He swam toward me.

"Get Pilo, I couldn't hold on to him."

"I'll get you both," Pontius said as he grabbed my arm and swam toward Pilo.

"My clothing is too wet. It's dragging me down."

"Take it off."

"I can't."

"I'm on shore now," Pilo called to us.

"Good boy, Pilo. Stay there. We are coming," Pontius said to him.

"Pontius, I can't move. It is just too heavy."

"Here, get on my back. Hold on."

I wrapped my arms around his shoulders. He slowly made his way to where Pilo stood on the shore. In the evening light, I could see the figure of a big man standing with Pilo. I was frightened, who was it?

"Can you two make it?" The man called to us.

"Yes. Who are you?" I replied.

"Simon Peter."

I relaxed.

Pontius made it to shore. Peter reached down and pulled me up. Pontius climbed up on his own.

"Are we glad to see you, Peter," Pontius said as he embraced the Lord's Apostle.

"The Lord bid that I should come here and help you. Please, we must hurry. We have a safe place for you to hide."

"Peter, our daughters are still back at the villa, I don't think that Claudius knows about them. We must get them," Pontius told him.

"Don't worry. They are safe with us. Gaius got them after we learned that the three of you were taken."

"Oh, thank you," I said.

"I have a cart on the road. We'll have a bit of a ride to where we live."

When we got to the cart, Peter had blankets for us. He put us under them not just to keep us warm but to hide us.

I held Pilo close to me. He shivered. Pontius squeezed my hand. We were safe for now.

I whispered a prayer, "Thank you, Lord."

58. New Life

Somewhere in Rome

THE CART RATTLED OVER THE PAVING STONES. I glanced at Claudia, who held our shivering son. The warm blanket covered us, but I feared Pilo wasn't just shaking from the cold. Our ten-year-old son had just faced death and saw something a boy his age should never see, an executioner about to kill his parents. I stroked his hair. He looked at me, the tears cascaded down his face.

Yeshua, I know you hear me, wherever you are, I thank you for preserving the life of my family. I cannot express in words, my deepest gratitude. I certainly don't deserve your constant kindness, Claudia and Pilo do, they have always believed.

I'm not sure how much time passed before the cart came to a halt but when Peter pulled back the blanket we were in what appeared to be a cave.

"You can get out of the cart now. You are safe. This is where the Lord's community in Rome lives."

Peter lifted Pilo and Claudia off the cart and extended a helping hand to me. We were still wet but not as cold. As we started to walk into the cave, Gaius met us, he was carrying our daughters. Little Claudia ran to her mother, and I wrapped Myriam in my arms. We were whole again.

"Thank you, Gaius. Did you encounter any trouble?" I asked him.

"No. I expect the officials will wait until morning to take possession of your villa. I told your servants to get out as quickly as they could. They declined to come with me."

"Thank you for seeing to them. I owe them so much, and I don't just mean wages."

Gaius nodded.

We entered a large room with a fire pit burning in the center and food cooking over it. The walls had alcoves with blankets and pillows in them. I surmised that they were beds.

I counted forty people living in the cave. Some were eating, others were carrying on discussions. Peter called them together.

"Brothers and sisters, please welcome these people to our community. Some of you know them as you have been their providers. This is Pontius Pilate, Claudia, Pilo, little Claudia, and Myriam. On this day, the Lord preserved their lives and brought them to us."

The people clapped and came forward to greet us.

"We will get you some dry clothing so you can get out of those wet ones," one woman said.

"Please, come and have supper," another offered.

Peter smiled at all the attention we were getting. He almost seemed like a proud father.

"Do all your community members live here? I asked him.

"No. Only those who are in the most danger of being unfairly treated by authorities," he replied.

"Like us."

"You are free to stay with us as long as you are in need."

"Thank you, Peter."

I was handed a plate of supper consisting of fish and vegetables. I started to eat but was interrupted by a prayer of thanksgiving. I joined them in the *Amen.*

***

Claudia and the children had bedded down in the alcoves. They were sleeping peacefully. I was too filled with anxiety to sleep. I sat with my head against the wall of the cave. Peter and Gaius were keeping me company.

No conversation transpired between us, I think they were waiting for me to speak. I watched the flames in the fire pit. It had a calming effect on me. The shock of the day eased.

My eyes glanced around the room. I saw a passageway to another opening in the cave, I assumed it was another room.

"Where does that passage go?" I asked Peter.

He replied, "To the cisterns. One is for drinking water, the other is for baptisms."

Baptism. I refused it the last time he offered it to me.

"Peter, is it too late for me?"

"It's never too late. Do you want baptism?"

"Yes. It's time."

"Come. The Waters of New Life are waiting for you."

Gaius had a big smile on his face.

I followed Peter through the narrow passage to the cistern room. He slipped off his clothing and invited me to do the same. I stepped into the frigid water up to my waist.

"Maybe I should have accepted this baptism in Cornelius' warm pool when I had a chance," I said.

The two of them laughed at me. "It won't take long," Peter replied.

Peter took up a position slightly behind me and to my right. He put his arm behind me and gripped my left shoulder.

"Hold your nose and lean against my arm."

He pulled me down into the water three times saying the words, "I baptize you, Pontius Pilate, in the name of the Father, and of the Son, and of the Holy Spirit,"

On the third time I came up from the water, I felt a familiar warm breeze blow around me. "You've got me," I said.

I heard the Lord speak, *Peace be with you, my friend.* At that moment, I felt warm; all the anxiety and tension melt away. I was at peace. I wiped the water from my face and embraced the fisherman. The darkness I had been feeling for so long was gone.

The Lord preserved my life that day and gave me a new life. The date was engraved on my heart: *25.06. Year One of The Reign of Claudius.*

***

Being in a cave made it difficult to know the time of day. When I woke, I wasn't sure if it was morning. I could smell something cooking, so I figured it was breakfast. I rolled over in my alcove and was greeted by my wife holding a fresh biscuit.

"Good morning, husband. Are you hungry?"

"I sure am if that tastes as good as it smells."

I sat up and devoured my wife's offering.

"I see our children have found some friends."

"Yes, they sure have. They've been running around here all morning. I'm surprised they didn't wake you."

"I had a great sleep. It's nice to see Pilo having fun. I was worried about him after yesterday."

"I was concerned about all of us," Claudia said.

"I accepted baptism last night."

Claudia threw her arms around me. "Oh, Pontius, I'm so happy for you. That's marvelous."

"Yes. I am feeling a great sense of peace."

"The Lord loves you. And so do I."

"I can't image being without either one of you."

Claudia climbed into the alcove with me, even though it was a little small for two, we managed.

"You know, dear, we have to think about what we are going to do. We can't stay here. Our children need a home," I said.

"I been thinking about that. My uncle had a place in Gallia near Vienna. I went there as a child to visit in the summer. He left it to me when he died. It is a big place with orchards and a vineyard. There are some smaller guest houses on the property. What do you think?" Claudia told me.

"Sounds like it might be suitable. We just have to get there."

***

I went in search of Peter. I strolled to the cave entrance. Peter and Gaius were unloading supplies from the cart.

"Good Morning. You have risen," Peter said smiling at me.

"You are looking well for a dead person," Gaius added.

"Dead?"

"Well, that's the story around town. The executioner and the guard swore to Claudius that they completed their task and that your bodies were thrown into the river."

I thought for a moment and then it occurred to me. "They didn't want to admit that we got away, or they would lose their heads."

"Exactly. So nobody is looking for you. That's the good news. The bad news is Claudius has ordered that the Ponti estate be turned over to him., so you're poor and homeless," Gaius said.

"My wife isn't though."

"Oh, how's that?"

"We were just discussing what we should do about our living situation and Claudia told me that she has inherited a place with a vineyard and orchard near Vienna in Gallia. We think it would be a good place for the children and we would be out of harm's way."

Gaius smiled at me. "Have you ever made wine?"

"No, but I know how to drink it."

Peter threw a sack of flour at me. I almost caught it. "How about bread, can you make bread?"

"No, but I'm sure Claudia can."

Peter and Gaius laughed.

"Well, before you rush off to Gallia, It is essential for you learned about the importance of bread and wine in your new life as a Christian," Peter said.

"You know, I remember Yeshua wrote about that on the scrolls. It happened just after you refused to let him wash your feet."

"What scrolls? What are you talking about?" Peter said as he creased his forehead.

"During one of his visits with me, he suggested that the two of us to write our experience of the days before, during and after his death."

"He…wrote…it… down?" Peter asked. He jumped off the cart.

"Yes."

"Where are these scrolls? At your villa?"

"No. We didn't have a chance to bring them. Cornelius took the scrolls. He put them with the shroud for safe keeping."

"Pontius…the Lord's shroud? How did he get that?"

"We went to his tomb to investigate the resurrection story. I ordered Cornelius to destroy it, but he didn't."

Peter sat down on the cart, mouth open and rubbing his beard in disbelief.

"There's too great a risk to have him send them. I wish I had known about this before my family left Judea. They are due in port here tomorrow, along with Gaius' family."

"I'm sorry, I didn't realize they would be of value to anyone except me."

"How much did he write?'

"Everything he did right up to when he left for his kingdom. He went to a hill in Bethany. After that, it's just me recollecting until Shavuot."

"Will you tell me about this bread and wine thing he did? I didn't understand what he was doing, it seemed odd."

"It was strange to us at the time too, but it was all made clear when we received the Holy Spirit. Of course, I'll share it with you. You will need it for your life's journey."

***

The Next Day

Gaius and Peter helped us load the cart with enough food for us to make it to Vienna. My mind was still reeling from the revelation at the celebration of the Lord's Supper. *He knew.*

At supper last evening, Peter said the Lord's word over some flat bread and a cup of wine. It wasn't until I consumed them that I understood the significance of what we were doing. Peter gave me some flat bread and wine and told me to perform the same ritual for my family and any other Christian we meet on our journey.

"I wish you all well. May the Lord bless and keep you safe in him," Peter said.

The community gave us one of their carts and a mule. They had been so accepting and kind to us that was hard to leave.

We embraced everyone.

When I got to Gaius, I could feel the emotions welling up. That man had saved my life and that of my family more often than I could count. We stared at each for an uncomfortable few moments; two hardened Roman soldiers whose lives had been radically altered. Men who had been brought to their knees by a man who died and was alive again.

"Gaius, it has occurred to me that I never apologized for my behavior toward you the day of the battle. I am sorry."

He pulled his arm across his chest and said, "Apology accepted, sir. Let us not think of it again."

We embraced. I boarded the cart with my family, I took the reins and slapped the mule to pull. We headed northwest. It would take two weeks to get to Vienna.

Rome thought of me as dead, but I was alive and born again.

Epilog 64 A.D.

Vienna, Gallia

Greetings from Pontius Pilate.

THERE ARE EVENTS IN EVERYONE'S LIFE, I think, when something happens, a decision is taken, or someone enters your life for just a few minutes or hours, and it creates a massive shift in your direction even though you are not aware of it at the time. This is what happened to me hours before the Jewish Passover Feast in the seventh year of my tenure as Prefect of Judea.

I was told by the court astrologers the earth shifted that day. The blood red sun and the earthquake were signs, they said, that all the gods were angry. They warned me that the gods would avenge the fact that I had killed one of their own. My wife Claudia and son Pilo had turned away from me. I was alone in the Praetorium with the Galilean's bloody footprints.

The deed hung over me like an executioner's sword. Perhaps death at the hands of Tiberius would have been the better option, but at the time, the thought of letting justice prevail evaporated as concern for self-preservation darkened my soul.

The scrolls, on which the one I sent to the cross that day tells his part of the story and I tell mine, are in safe keeping. For your reading, I have transcribed what is written on them. I swear to you this is the truth.

Ecce homo est vivens. Behold the man is alive.

Who Are They?

Yeshua – Jesus of Nazareth's Hebrew name.

Pontius Pilate – Prefect of Judea 26 A. D. to 37 A.D. He was appointed by Tiberius and deposed by the Legat of Syria on complaints by the Samaritans.

Claudia Procula – Wife of Pontius Pilate. She is mentioned in the Gospel of Matthew but is not named. Her name developed over time from anecdotal evidence, which also linked her as the granddaughter of Augustus and illegitimate daughter of Tiberius.

Pilo – the son of Pilate and Claudia. His name is found is the writings of Claudia. He had clubbed foot, which was healed by Jesus though not at the moment indicated in this story.

Centurion Cornelius - Mention in the Acts of the Apostles as the first non-Jew to be baptized. He was stationed in Caesarea and was head of the Italia guard, which served to protect the prefects/governors. He was later made the first bishop of Caesarea.

Centurion Gaius Marius – Composite character. The centurion whose servant Jesus healed and the centurion who declared at the foot of the cross, "Surely, this man was the Son of God." The Third Letter of John is addressed to a 'Gaius'(3Jn 1:1)

Commander Marcus Rufus – His name is found the Letter of Pontius Pilate to Seneca the Younger. He commanded the forces under Pilate.

Joanna – Disciple of Jesus. In Luke's Gospel, she is mention as among the women who served Jesus and provided for his mission. She was married to Chuza a steward in Herod's court.

Alexander Pilate's Secretary – His name is found in the Letter of Pontius Pilate to Seneca.

Lazarus, Martha, and Mary – Friends of Jesus. They lived in Bethany just outside Jerusalem. Jesus frequented their home, "the house of Martha". It was Mary of Bethany who anointed the feet of Jesus at a dinner in Bethany in John's Gospel. Jesus raised Lazarus from the dead. Their novel is *Larazus of Bethany*.

Author's Notes.

This novel is a strictly fictional storyline of Pontius Pilate and his wife and their relationship with Jesus of Nazareth.

These notes are presented here for the reader's interest.

The Ethiopian Orthodox Tewahedo Church recognized **Pontius Pilate as a saint in the 6th century.** This designation is based on the account in the Acts of Pilate (Now called the Gospel of Nicodemus). The church also recognizes his wife, Claudia Procula, whose dream of Christ caused her to write a note to Pilate to stop him from crucifying Jesus. **Their feast day is June 25**.

The Greek Church names Claudia as a saint. **Her day is Oct 27**.

Further Readings

The Apocryphal Gospels, Acts, and Revelations translated by Alexander Walker. Published in 1870, digitized by Google from the library of Harvard University. Also held in the Vatican Library. The following are of interest:

1. Gospel of Nicodemus

2. The Letter of Pontius Pilate to Tiberius

3. The Report of Pilate, the Procurator concerning Our Lord Jesus Christ, sent to Rome to Tiberius Caesar

4. The Giving up of Pontius Pilate

5. The Death of Pilate

6. The Gospel of James

Relics of Repentance: The Letters of Pontius Pilate and Claudia Procula, Published by Issana Press, 1996 and 2002

The Letters of Herod and Pilate: The Lost Books of the Bible [1926], at sacred-texts.com

Tid Bits

According to the Apocryphal document, *The Report of Pilate the Procurator to Caesar*, "my soldiers were paid-off to change their story. However, they kept the money but did not keep their silence about what they had witnessed." (at the tomb of Jesus)

Mare Nostrum is Latin for "Our Sea" the name ancient Romans gave to the Mediterranean Sea

Early in his tenure as prefect, Pilate brought banners of Tiberius to Jerusalem. The Jews considered it an affront to the Holy City. A protest took place, and Pilate threatened to kill the men gathered in his courtyard in Caesarea. He refused to remove the banners from Jerusalem. When he sent the soldiers to kill the protesting Jews, the Jews knelt and bared their necks to the soldiers. Pilate backed off. He ordered the soldier to their barracks and removed the banners from Jerusalem.

Another protest took place in Jerusalem against Pilate using the Temple funds to finance the aqueduct. His usage of the funds was not illegal, and the Sanhedrin approved of the funding. They later backed the accusation that Pilate took the money. The protest turned violent. Even though Pilate ordered the soldiers not to use their swords, they did. As a result, many people were injured or died.

About the Author:

E. Ann McIntyre is a Catholic Christian writer who focuses on the people in the Gospels and brings them to life in their own spiritual journeys. *Feast of Pontius Pilate* is one such story. There is one person who is present in each of her novels – Yeshua.

Other novels by Ms. McIntyre includes *Lazarus of Bethany* and *Yes, a Story Story*.

You can find a complete list of her writings and links to purchase them at https://McIntyreOnlinePublishing.ca

Contact: elizabethanne@mcintyreonlinepublishing.ca

Twitter: Ann McIntyre @mcian157